THE BANSHEE'S SPARK

THE PARANORMAL COUNCIL #9

LAURA GREENWOOD

What if you knew who your mate was, but you couldn't touch them?

Reese and Faye have known they were meant to be together since they were five years old. But even holding hands is painful for them, and they've never taken things any further as a result. When care-free Penny turns up, things begin to change, and if they can avoid the Witch Hunters that are after Faye's family, then maybe they can finally have a chance for a happily ever after...

-

The Banshee's Spark is part of the Paranormal Council series and is Faye, Reese, and Penny's complete series.

FAYE FINISHED PLAITING her hair and looked in the mirror with a sigh. One more day done. God knew how many more to go. Sometimes she didn't think she'd be able to hold out any longer, but then there was always something that changed her mind. Now, it was her eldest sister's surprise daughter. Fiona was unbelievably cute, but she made Faye's heart ache in ways she didn't want to spend too long thinking about. She wanted a family of her own so badly. But considering she couldn't even touch her mate without feeling excruciating pain, it didn't seem likely at any point soon. She'd talked to others about it, but the only people she knew who were mated but hadn't touched for years were Eira and Josh, but they both said it'd never been painful. Which meant it was just her and Reese that had to deal with it this way.

Slowly, she regained her composure, leaving the bathroom and entering the bedroom they tortured themselves further by sharing. At least they had separate beds, she didn't think she could avoid touching him if they shared.

He was standing there, looking as delicious and touchable as always. Which was part of the problem. She longed for him. Yearned for him even, but there was nothing she could do to actually make that yearning a reality. He'd never be able to run his hand down her back, even through clothing. He'd never be able to kiss her properly. They'd never be able to....

Faye shook her head, desperate to rid herself of the thoughts assailing her. They'd only grown worse since her sister, Mia, had met her mate. Watching the short affectionate touches she exchanged with Felix was almost as painful as any attempt to touch Reese.

"Faye," he said softly. "Please stop torturing yourself."

"I can't," she said, her voice almost breaking, and tears threatened in the corners of her eyes.

"I just want to be able to touch you, to be with you."

"I know. I feel it too. But I'm here, I'm not going anywhere." He reached out a hand, before dropping it back to his side, realising what he was doing. Their relationship had always been like this. Natural reactions to situations, followed by the swift realisation that they couldn't go through with it.

"I know, but..." She glanced away, already hating how weak she felt about the whole thing. Why wasn't she used to it? She'd have thought that after all this time she'd have realised they couldn't have what normal couples did. There'd be no lingering kisses good night, or stray hand brushing against an arm and offering comfort. Nor would there be any of the true intimacy they needed.

And there'd never be a family. Well, she supposed that wasn't true. They could always adopt, or have some kind of IVF, though if it would work on witches, she had no idea. But there'd never be a family that was just theirs. No child who was the perfect combination of her and Reese.

"Faye, please," he begged, stepping forward despite the knowledge he couldn't comfort her.

She shook her head and moved backwards, her

back hitting the wall and her lip quivering with emotion. Here would be the perfect opportunity for a kiss, while he caged her against the wall and pushed himself against her.

She bit her lip, a soft whimper escaping. Why did she do this to herself? It wasn't like it could go anywhere. And it wasn't like she'd actually know what she was doing if they *did* go further. That was the big problem with having known her mate since they were both small. Well, and not being able to touch him. It didn't exactly bode well for intimate moments. So she'd reached her twenties and was still pretty much clueless when it came to sex.

Unless she counted the times she touched herself in the middle of the night, imagining all the things Reese would do to her if he could. Or the things she hoped he would.

"What are you thinking, Faye?"

"Huh?" she responded instantly, taken aback by his question.

"What's going through your pretty little head? You're making sounds like you do when you think I'm asleep," he teased, taking a step forward, crowding her against the wall and actually caging her there, just like she'd imagined him doing. She swallowed audibly, affected far more than she wanted to admit by his mere proximity.

"Erm..."

"Are you imaging the things I'd do to you, Faye?" he asked, his voice low and sultry. "You don't have to imagine. I'm happy to tell you."

"Oh."

He leaned in close, his mouth hovering just next to her ear. She could feel his breath fanning over her skin, and longed for more. To feel his lips touch. Knowing that it wasn't even a possibility, only made her more aware of what was going on, and more desperate to actually do things. Damn, life really wasn't fair.

"Come back to me, Faye," he whispered. "You've gone away to worry, I can tell."

"Sorry," she murmured, looking up into his beautiful brown eyes. A lot of people found them a little unnerving, but that was just his bird side coming through. But she was used to it, and it hadn't bothered her in years. If it ever actually had. She wasn't completely convinced she had, it'd been that long since they'd met.

He lifted his hand so that it was hovering just next to her cheek, and she longed for him to close that gap, even if it would hurt. Especially because it would hurt. It would remind her of all the reasons why she shouldn't allow things to get that far.

"Touch me," she whispered, not regretting the words in the slightest. Worry clouded Reese's eyes.

"Are you sure?" His voice was soft, kind of reverent. He always got like this when she asked him. And it was always her that asked him, not the other way around. She didn't think it was because he didn't want to. More that he was more conscious of what it actually cost them to touch. Or he just had more restraint than she did.

"Yes." She channelled as much begging into her eyes as possible, and it evidently worked, as Reese lowered his hand the rest of the way and touched her cheek with one gentle finger.

There was probably about a second of enjoyment before the pain hit. Sharp needles dancing across her cheek, around where their skin touched, but spreading out even further. The worst bit was that it wasn't just skin on skin that was the problem. They'd tried using gloves, but the result had been the same. It was more to do with there being any connection at all.

Reese pulled away as a single spark ignited before Faye's eyes, and fell to the floor, fading as it went. Just another reason she knew that there was something wrong with their bond. She sparked, just like other witches did when they touched their mates, but it was only one, and only lasted for a moment, before fading into nothingness.

She could live with it. So long as their bond didn't do the same.

2

PENNY ALMOST SKIPPED out of the bakery, taking a large bite of her pastry as she did. She got a funny look from a passing business woman, but shrugged it off. She ran daily, she deserved a damn pastry, even if she was still in her workout gear.

Running daily was a little bit of an understatement. She pretty much exercised all day, every day, which was unsurprising given she was a yoga instructor.

The walk to her studio was only a short one, but she still enjoyed it as a good cool down. Even so, she was looking forward to a hot coffee when she got in. It was really the only way to perk her up.

She was humming along to herself, in a complete world of her own, and almost ran into the woman waiting outside the door. She jumped back, thankful she hadn't gotten a take-out coffee, otherwise it'd have ended up all over her, and that would never do.

"I'm so sorry," the woman said, reaching out a hand to try and steady Penny, even though she hadn't actually fallen.

"No need to be sorry," Penny said, flashing her a beaming smile while studying the woman in front of her.

She was slim, but curvy, with wavy dishwater blonde hair that framed her face. But it was the other woman's eyes that got Penny the most. They were so sad. Like the sorrow of a hundred people lived in her. Something within Penny longed to make her feel better. There was just a part of her that felt like the woman was calling out to her. So much so, that she nearly reached out to touch her, but pulled back at the last second. Mostly because it would be a bit weird to do that to a stranger, and the last thing she wanted was to make the wrong impression on someone she didn't know.

"Can I help you?" Penny asked, flashing another smile. Yes, this woman was calling to her, in a way that no one ever really had before. Penny had never minded if the people she went for were male or female, so long as there was some kind of connection between them. Even so. It all paled in comparison to the reaction the blonde was having on her.

"Oh, sorry. I'm Faye, I'm here for the yoga session. I think."

"You think?" Penny laughed a little, but mostly to hide the effect that Faye's name had on her. She was heating up all over, and if that was what a name would do, she dreaded to think what other things would.

"Sorry, yes, I am."

"Do you always apologise so much?" she asked, cocking her head to the side and watching as Faye chewed on her bottom lip.

"No," the other woman admitted.

"Huh."

"But I *am* here for yoga. It helps with stress, right?" She looked hopeful, like there was far more resting on this than just the release of life's daily stresses. Penny looked her up and down again, appreciating the long toned legs that were already clad in workout gear. She'd relieve this woman's tension any day. Catching the thought, she scolded herself. That wasn't acceptable to think about anyone. Particularly someone she didn't know. What was wrong with her today?

"I just need to open up and grab myself a coffee,

but the class starts in maybe half an hour." She pulled the key to the building out of her bag and slipped it into the lock, the action really not helping with the direction her thoughts were taking. Seemed her mind was really in the gutter.

"Oh, I'm early?" Faye seemed hesitant, like she really wasn't sure of herself. It was endearing.

"A little bit, I must have listed the time wrong on the website."

"I don't think you did," she sounded more certain this time, which was interesting. Seemed that when she was defending someone, her fight came back. Or just came to front, Penny guessed. Technically, she'd not had any fight at all up until now, so it couldn't come back. Odd thought there. It was almost as if Penny already knew the woman. Which didn't make *any* sense. She'd have remembered if she'd met this blonde beauty before.

"How can you be so sure?" Penny teased, knowing full well the time on the website were correct. She checked them almost daily as a force of habit. Mostly to avoid this kind of situation happening. Though she wasn't going to complain too much.

"I like to be early," Faye muttered, looking away. Okay, so there was clearly something else going on there. Maybe if she got the woman a drink, and took her into the yoga room, she could get her to relax and tell her more.

"I get that." She opened the door, and waved the blonde through, pleased when she didn't protest and made her way into the building that was dark, cold, and smelled of stale sweat. On second thoughts, maybe it wasn't the best place to take her.

"Oh, it reminds me of dance lessons," Faye said, looking around the hall as Penny turned the light on.

"You dance?" Penny's heart leaped. Next to yoga, dance was what she'd wished she could do. There was something about the grace of the body moving that she just loved and appreciated.

"I used to." Faye trailed her hand over the bar along the side of the room. It wasn't used much, from what Penny could tell, only when the little children came for their ballet lessons. She'd watched once, and her heart had melted. She'd love kids one day, but they weren't possible for her kind. Not even with her mate, which sucked spectacularly.

Her eyes wandered back to Faye, watching intently. Mate felt like a much more comfortable word than it normally did, and she found she liked it.

"Why did you stop?"

"It hurt." Faye's answer stopped any hint at more

of a conversation. There was just something about it that hinted at more, and Penny longed to ask, but also didn't dare.

"Have you tried since?"

"No. I keep meaning to, but..." She looked up, meeting Penny's eyes with her own. There was a lingering pain there. Not one that would be easily chased away. Not at all. This was a pain that was added to daily and never ceased. A pain that would take time to erase. One that Penny longed to. "I need to go," Faye muttered, turning to flee from the room. She brushed passed Penny, and she could've sworn she saw a couple of sparks ignite around where they touched. But no, that couldn't be possible.

She watched the other woman running into the distance, and it was only once she'd left that Penny noticed she'd left her phone behind.

She scooped it up, intending just to check if there was somewhere she could return it to. But she noticed the message on the screen before she could help herself.

Reese: *Faye, please come home. We can talk about it.*

The name on the screen caused a fluttering in her belly. Well, the names. She couldn't actually identify where her feelings started and ended when it came to what was there. Which was odd. Normally she was so sure of herself.

One thing was sure though, she needed to call this Reese, even if it was just so she had an excuse to see Faye again. They were clearly an item after all.

3

"Faye, what's wrong?" he asked, trying to keep the frown from marring his features. If she saw that, then she'd likely only end up more worried. He'd known Faye, and been with her, long enough to know that was how she'd react to him doing that.

"Nothing."

She was agitated. It was probably a bad idea for him to do or say anything, yet he couldn't leave it be, she meant too much to him for that. And, when he couldn't comfort her with a hug, he had to actually say things.

"Faye, stop. Something is clearly bothering you. Talk to me?"

"I..."

He waited patiently, knowing that she needed that from him.

"I saw someone else that made me feel like you do," she said, the words so soft that he almost thought that they were a mistake. Or certainly not what she'd intended to say. It took him a few moments to actually process what she was saying, and he mulled the words over in his head a few times. Surprisingly, they didn't seem to be causing quite the reaction he thought they should. Instead of hating the words, he found them oddly comforting. Weird, but he'd deal with that revelation later.

"Okay, want to tell me about him?" he asked instead. Faye looked up, her eyes startled. Probably for the same reason he was surprised.

"Her," she said eventually. Reese arched an eyebrow. That just raised a whole new set of questions. "How should I know?" She flung her hands in the air before she collapsed onto their sofa, burying her head in her hands. He moved over to her instantly, and before he thought about it, he slipped an arm around her and pulled her close, taking in the scent of her shampoo as her head rested on his shoulder. The pain was almost instant, but he did his best to push it away. He hadn't told Faye, but he'd actually been practicing withstanding pain just so he could touch her. It was stupid really, mostly because it wouldn't help combat what she felt too, but he'd do anything so they could have a normal relationship.

Faye moved closer, clutching his shirt with her hand and taking in a long breath. Reese did the same, loving her closeness even if it hurt. But he said nothing. He didn't want to break the spell they were seemingly under. She sniffed, and he could tell tears were about to fall. Hesitantly, he stroked his hand through her hair, enjoying the silkiness of the strands through the pain.

It was worth it, no matter how much it hurt. Every stab of pain was worth it, just to touch her.

Eventually, it became a little too much, and he pulled his hand away.

"No, don't stop."

"Faye, I have to." His voice cracked as he spoke, the prolonged pain that was still assailing him where they touched, almost too much.

"Oh." She looked up briefly, before looking away again, probably to try not let him see the hurt that was in her eyes. "Oh," she said louder, pulling back. This time he could see her eyes a lot clearer, and couldn't miss the widened stare.

"Missing something?"

"It didn't hurt," she said, reverently.

"No." He couldn't stop the smile that spread across his face. She'd clearly been too wrapped up in their closeness to actually notice straight away.

"But it hurt you?" She frowned, and his heart swelled. There was something about the look she was giving him that just filled him with a happy content feeling.

"Yes, it still hurt me," he replied. It was confusing, but anything was progress in his mind, especially if it meant he and Faye could finally progress in their relationship. Maybe he could even ask her to marry him. Then again, after the disaster that'd been Bex's wedding, maybe not.

"Why?" Her eyes widened, and he longed to remove the hurt from them, maybe soon.

"I don't know," he answered, half-truthful. He had a good idea what the change was, but he didn't want to voice it until he was sure. Only problem was that he had no idea how to find out if he was right or not. In theory, all he'd have to do is find the woman Faye was talking about. Except, he had no idea where they'd met, what her name was, or anything else. He daren't ask Faye either, he didn't want to get her hopes up.

"Oh." She pushed herself up from the sofa, and he

already felt bereft at the loss of closeness. Even if they couldn't touch, he always felt more complete when she was near him. "Dinner?" she asked, breaking through his thoughts. He nodded once, and got up to help.

4

"FAYE, ARE YOU LISTENING?"

"Huh?" she asked her older sister. Well, her middle sister. Mia was between her and Bex in age.

"Obviously not. I'd ask if you were in love, but..."

"We all know Reese is it for me," she replied without thinking. Except now, she wasn't so sure. Images of the toned redhead from the day before assailed Faye's mind. Yes, she definitely wasn't so sure anymore. She shouldn't be feeling like that about anyone other than Reese, should she? She'd known they were meant to be mates since they were children, and her magic had sparked when they'd touched for the first time. Oh the blissful innocence of youth, when they could touch without the pain. It'd all stopped when they'd turned eighteen, though the arrival of Faye's familiar, in the shape of a raven, had stopped her from doubting that they were meant to be together. It all just added up towards one thing, he was hers.

"We do, yes. Now, I was trying to suggest you used this potion..."

"It won't work," Faye interrupted. She was grateful to Mia for trying, but there were some things she knew deep down were true. And one of them was that no amount of potions or spells was going to sort the problem she had. Magic would, but it wasn't the kind of magic that could be cast or brewed. It was a more fundamental magic that would be the answer. One that was entwined with the very nature of the universe itself.

The redhead crossed through Faye's mind again, and she shook her head to get rid of the image. How could she be thinking of another woman like that? She had Reese, and he was all she needed. Even if he couldn't give her some things.

"Will you at least try?" Mia asked, her eyes begging Faye, who sighed.

"Fine," she gave in, knowing it would likely be easier to do so than to listen to her sister berate her for the rest of the afternoon. She wasn't even sure why Mia had the afternoon off work. She really shouldn't. She wasn't like Faye, whose job as a makeup artist had weird hours. Instead, Mia worked in a lab, mixing things. That was where her sister's talents lay, in potions and other mixes. Faye's powers were far more subtle. More in line with the finer arts. She could use her magic to create stunning makeup, even some cake decorations. But what she wouldn't admit to anyone, was that she failed every time she tried to do any bigger magic.

When she'd been little, her eldest sister, Bex, had often done the spells underhandedly, then passed them off as Faye's work. She'd gotten lucky in the sister department. She glanced at Mia, who was scooping up potion from her cauldron and putting it into a small vial. The potion shined a light pink, and sparkled in the light. Yes, Faye was very lucky in the sister department, she didn't know how she could ever repay all the other two did for her.

"Here you go," Mia said, handing her the vial.

"Thanks," she muttered, slipping it into her pocket. "I still don't think it'll work."

"I know," Mia replied instantly, "but it's at least worth a try, Faye. Anything is better than seeing you in as much pain as you're in now."

"I'm not in pain," she insisted, the returning look

on Mia's face showing how little her sister believed her.

"Not physical pain maybe." Mia sighed. "Have you tried the necklace recently?" she changed tack.

"No. You know I..."

"Here."

Before Faye could protest further, a long jewellery box was thrust into her hand. She should've known Mia had this planned. She put a lot of stock in the necklaces their Grandmother had left them. In fact, Mia was wearing hers already, the stone nestled against her chest. She'd never admit it, but seeing the stone always made Faye a little jealous. She'd known her mate the longest, much longer than Mia had known Felix, and yet her own box was lying stubbornly unopened.

"Just try," Mia said.

"Fine, but only because it's you." And because it was easier to give into her, than it was to fight it. Slowly, and knowing what the outcome would be, Faye pressed the catch. She drew in a sharp breath and almost dropped it when the box opened for her, revealing a necklace just like Mia's, but with a slightly pinkish glow to the stone. "But..."

"Has something changed recently?" Mia asked, perceptive as always. Well, apart from the time she managed to accidentally get herself love potioned without realising it. If Faye wasn't so distracted right now, then she'd definitely be ribbing her sister over that.

"No, I...well yes."

"Which is it?" Mia smirked. Damn sisters. Always thinking they knew better.

"Yes. Something changed. Reese touched me last night, and it didn't hurt."

"That's great news!" Mia was practically bouncing up and down, making Faye smile. Her sister's happiness was a little infectious.

"Yes, and no."

"Now you're just being confusing. Do I need to set Bex on you?"

Faye let out an involuntary laugh. They both knew Bex wouldn't do anything. She couldn't deny her youngest sister's wishes. It seemed to go against her as a person. But also, she knew Mia wouldn't disturb her, not now they knew about Fiona. Mother and daughter were having some much needed, and deserved, time alone together.

"It still hurt Reese."

"But not you?" Mia frowned. Faye didn't blame her, it was confusing for her too, and it was the life she was actually living.

"Yes. Him but not me. It doesn't make any sense." She glanced away, hoping the other woman wouldn't see what she was hiding in her eyes.

"It's like Josh and Eira, isn't it?" Mia asked, referring to their friends. The two of them hadn't been able to touch until Eira had met her other two mates. But it was different. Or at least, Faye thought it was. It hadn't hurt either of them to actually touch, it had just been something Josh hadn't really wanted. He'd tried to explain it, but really, it was just a little confusing as far as Faye was concerned.

"Yes, no, I'm not sure. Is anyone like them?"

"Probably not," Mia admitted.

"So what's changed?"

Indecision warred within her as she considered whether to actually tell her or not. On the one hand, Mia might be able to help her work it out. There was no doubt her middle sister was smart after all. On the other, she didn't really want to admit the possibility of there being someone else.

"Spill, Faye. Now."

"I think I met someone else."

"Oh."

"Yes, oh." Faye looked away, before beginning to pace, particularly on edge by the situation. She really didn't know what was going on.

"How do you feel about that?"

"I don't know," Faye admitted. "It was odd."

"Did it feel right, though?"

"I suppose so."

"The necklace says so," Mia pointed out.

"I know, but..."

"But, what? Are you seriously trying to avoid what feels right? You should know better than that, especially after my situation with Skyler."

"Mmm." Faye wasn't quite sure what to say to that one. "Have you heard anything more about him?" she asked instead, thinking about the man who'd managed to dupe her sister. And by dupe, she meant kidnap.

"No." Mia sighed. "Absolutely nothing. Robert's a mess, but that's to be expected. Weirdly, I think he actually cares for Bex, just not in the way we thought."

"He'd better do," Faye almost growled. Thinking about the human man who was technically married to their eldest sister always did that to her. It didn't even matter that Robert and Bex's marriage was in name only, and always had been. He set Faye all kinds of on edge.

"He does, I think. He wants to protect her and Fiona."

"Not enough to stop Mia getting..."

"I know, Faye, I know." A shadow crossed the dark haired woman's face as she thought back over all that had occurred. Faye knew Mia hadn't been imprisoned for long. Maybe an hour or so, but the things she'd seen had scarred her. Not that she'd talked about it. A part of Faye was dying to know, and wanted to ask about it. The other part of her knew that Mia would talk in her own time, and only when she was ready.

"But, no. Nothing about Skyler. Or whatever weird association he belonged to." She shivered.

"You don't think the witch hunters are back do you?" Faye asked, thinking back to Reagan's weird prophecy. Or vision, or whatever it was called. None of Faye's family were blessed with the sight. In fact, there was only Reagan she knew who had it at all. But their friend seemed to know things. Things that didn't bode well for the witches they knew.

"I don't think they ever really went away," Mia replied, busying herself with some papers that'd been left on one of the sides.

"What makes you say that?" She was curious. But also grateful for the change in subject. She hated talking about what was going on with her and Reese, and even more so now she had the redhead on her mind. Talking about something else, even if that was serious and potentially deadly.

"No one is that set up without centuries of funding and infrastructure." Another haunted look crossed Mia's eyes, and it was on the tip of Faye's tongue to ask more.

"I'm back," Felix's voice rang out through the hall. Mia let out an excited scream.

"That's my cue to go," Faye muttered.

"Why don't you like him?" Mia demanded, already getting defensive over her mate. Though she'd hate knowing that was how Faye referred to him. Mate was definitely a shifter word. Well, and a vampire one. Mia and Felix were neither. But Faye's mate *was* a shifter, so the term had kind of stuck in her mind.

"I don't have a problem with him," she insisted. Mostly because it was the truth. Felix was fine. In fact, Felix was lovely. He'd never been anything but kind to Faye, and the lengths he'd gone to just days after meeting Mia, had solidified her opinion of him. But watching the two of them together was painful. The lingering touches and soft looks were so at odds with her own relationship of avoiding touches and pained glances.

"Oh," Mia responded, understanding dawning

over her face. "I get it. Go, now." She leaned forward and pressed a soft kiss to Faye's cheek.

"I'll see you on Saturday?" she asked, receiving a nod in return.

"Every single week."

Faye joined in Mia's light laughter. She had a point. Their parents were nothing if not creatures of habit. They had lunch every Saturday, and expected their daughters, and their pluses, to always attend. Faye had enjoyed the lunches when it had just been the six of them, and she still did a little now. But Mia and Felix, and Bex and Fiona, made it a little more difficult for her to relax. Particularly when Reese sat beside her so stiffly as he resisted the urge to brush his hand against hers.

"See you then!" Mia called as Faye left the room, completely preoccupied by the idea of her redhead, and what that meant for her and Reese.

5

PENNY STARED AT THE PHONE. She wasn't sure whether she should be doing this, but curiosity was, without a doubt, going to get the better of her. She wanted to know more about the blonde. And wanted to know more about the person she seemed to be with.

She sucked in a deep breath, and pushed her long red hair behind her ear. Without thinking anymore about it, she pressed the call button. She chewed on her lip as she listened to the dial tone, half wanting the other person, who'd been listed in the phone as Reese, not to pick up. It would certainly avoid some of the awkward conversation they might have to have.

"Faye? Is everything okay?" The man's voice sent

a thrill through Penny, one she hadn't experienced in years. One that she'd never really experienced with men.

"Hi, is this Reese?" she asked, surprised by how easily his name slipped from her lips.

"Yes? Who is this? Why do you have Faye's phone?" His voice hardened.

"She left it with me yesterday," Penny answered, her voice shaking a little with nerves. Oh damn, that wasn't good. She never really got nervous, but talking to this man had her almost shaking.

"And you are..."

"Penny. Well, Penelope, but everyone calls me Penny," she blurted out, before cursing to herself. What the hell was wrong with her? She wasn't normally a mess like this. Then again, she normally wasn't interested enough in people for this. They were all great to look at and all, particularly if they were topless with hot streams of water flowing down their chests, but the rest of them? They didn't really get Penny's motor running. Yet this man, Reese, was. Just by talking to her as well. And he wasn't even saying anything that should be eliciting any kind of response in her, never mind the slight tightening in her chest as he spoke.

"Penny," he repeated, as if just trying out how her name sounded.

"Yes, Penny." She gulped loudly, then hoped he hadn't heard. That would be embarrassing and a half.

"And you met Faye yesterday?" He seemed hesitant this time, as if something in his question mattered a great deal to him. And maybe even to Faye. Maybe the blonde woman had talked about Penny when she'd seen him later. The thought filled her with an odd sense of satisfaction, until she realised she was still on the phone, and couldn't be thinking about things like that. She shouldn't be thinking about them anyway. Neither Faye, nor Reese, were hers to fantasise about. And even if they were, she couldn't. That would mean them finding out what she was, and the scorn that would, without a doubt, follow.

"Yes," she answered, hoping none of her insecurities showed.

"Hmm."

Penny waited for him to continue. There was little else she could do. She didn't know him well enough to respond to just a sound. Maybe in a little while...no. She couldn't think like that. He already belonged to Faye, not to her.

"Would you like to come for dinner tonight?" Reese asked after a pause.

"What?" She responded far more sharply than she intended, but his question had taken her well and truly off guard. Dinner? That was almost date sounding.

"Dinner. The meal at the end of the day, where three people can sit down and talk?" He chuckled, clearly amused by her confusion.

"But why?" She would admit to the confusion. Why should this man want her to come around for dinner? And he'd said three, which suggested Faye would be there too. Then again, she could think of far worse situations to be in than dinner with the blonde and the owner of the voice at the end of the phone.

"Call it a hunch, but I think it'll be a good idea," Reese said, and she could almost hear the shrug he was surely doing as he did so. "Plus, you have Faye's phone, she's probably panicking about not having it already."

"Oh, right, yes."

"Is that a yes to dinner?" he asked, still sounding amused.

"Yes." The word slipped out before she really intended it to, but even so, it felt right. There was just something about him, about the situation, that was calling to her.

"Good. See you at seven?"

"Sure."

"See you then, Penny." She liked the way her name sounded from him, almost so much that she nearly forgot one, key, piece of information.

"Where am I coming to?"

"I'll text you."

"You don't have my number."

"I'll text Faye's," he pointed out and she made an odd noise. She wasn't sure how she felt about reading the other woman's texts, even if it was accidental. "Don't worry, there's nothing shocking on there," Reese said, chuckling away to himself.

"Are you sure?"

"I should hope so, we've been together since we were five."

Her heart sank, she hadn't expected that. Maybe a year or so, but even if the two of them were in their early twenties, and it was difficult to tell with paranormals anyway, then they'd been together for nearly two decades. She wasn't sure how she was going to reveal that she knew they were paranormals. Outing someone's species was generally frowned upon. Yet one more curse her kind had to endure. They could tell what someone was, just by looking at them. Faye had reeked of witch, meaning Reese was likely paranormal too. He'd have to be for them to have been together that long.

"Okay. Thanks," she muttered.

"Seven, Penny. At the address I send you."

"You got it," she replied half-heartedly. She wasn't sure how she was going to get through dinner. She had to go. She could feel the pull *to* go. But watching the two of them together was going to be painful.

"I look forward to it," he said, before hanging up the phone.

Penny shook her head, before pulling the phone away from her ear and staring at it. Within seconds, it lit up, and she eagerly swiped across the screen, despite the sadness welling up inside her. She was a sucker for pain it seemed.

Except that the message wasn't from Reese. Instead, it was from someone called Mia. Penny tried to click off it, she didn't want to intrude into Faye's messages, but something about it caught her attention: *Have you tried the potion yet? ;-) x*

Definitely a witch then. Penny had already been certain of that. But what kind of potion was this Mia referring to? Maybe it was a love potion, and Reese wasn't actually Faye's mate, but rather someone who just thought he was. She was sure it didn't actually work like that, but hope welled up inside Penny.

So much so, that the moment Reese's text with the actual address popped up, she was in her car and planning what she was wearing for the evening. All she needed to do now, was find it. And then get through the following three hours until it was time for them to have dinner. And find out some answers. She hoped, anyway.

6

WHAT HAD REESE BEEN THINKING? The words had been going round and round in Faye's head ever since the redhead sat opposite her had arrived. At least she had her phone back? But that was hardly any consolation given the circumstances. Namely that she couldn't keep her eyes off the woman. Penny. Her name was Penny.

It suited her. Probably due to the coppery shade of her hair. Or maybe she was good luck, and all Faye had to do was pick her up. She laughed softly to herself, drawing a curious look from Reese. She dismissed it. Let him be curious, he'd brought this situation on himself when he'd invited someone for dinner without actually checking with her first. Not that she'd have been able to say no. She couldn't, and didn't want, to deny Reese anything. Especially with so much being off limits to them anyway.

"Can you pass the salt please?" Penny asked, smiling sweetly. Both Reese and Faye reached for the salt pot, that was seated half way between them. Their fingers brushed, and Faye sucked in a deep breath, preparing herself for the shooting pain that was to come. Except it didn't. Of course it didn't. *She* hadn't felt any pain at all since yesterday. They'd touched briefly again before bed the night before, and then again in the morning, just to check whether or not it'd been a fluke. Faye wasn't sure whether she was glad it wasn't, or annoyed. Reese still felt pain, so what was the point? She now wanted to touch him even more, but knew she couldn't because it'd hurt him.

"Are the two of you okay?" Penny's voice broke through the haze Faye had found herself in. Her voice had a musical quality to it, that tickled Faye's mind in an entirely pleasant way. She could get used to listening to that.

"Yes, sorry," Faye muttered, passing her the salt once Reese had let go.

"No," Reese said faintly, and the two women swivelled their heads to look at him.

"Reese?" Faye asked, moving her hand so it

hovered just over his. Offering comfort, but not touching him like would have been natural. They'd perfected the art of non-physical comfort.

"You can touch me, Faye," he whispered.

"Not worth the pain," she pointed out.

"There wasn't any."

"What?" She almost couldn't believe what he was saying. "Are you..."

Instead of saying anything, Reese pushed to his feet, and closed the small gap between his and Faye's chairs. They only had a small, circular, table, so it didn't take much doing. Unsure of what he was doing, Faye rose to her feet as well, meaning they were now stood just inches apart. His breathing was heavy, and she found her gaze settling on his lips. A lump formed in her throat and she swallowed down passed it. What was he up to? Was he intending to torture them both? Because as it stood, he was doing a damn good job of that.

"Reese?" she whispered.

His hand came to her cheek. Touching her. And he smoothed his thumb over her cheek. Even knowing she shouldn't, Faye leaned into his touch, enjoying the closeness. She enjoyed it even more when he leaned down and pressed his lips against hers.

For a moment, she was shocked. She'd imagined kissing Reese so often that she wasn't sure which fantasy she preferred. But all of those imaginings faded compared to this. This was...magical. She twined her arms around his neck, and pressed her body against his, deepening the kiss. Tingles began to build along her body, and she wondered if it wasn't just the touch thing that'd been sorted out, but her magic too. If Mia was to be believed, and the other witches she knew, then this was what was supposed to happen when they met their mate.

They broke apart, both breathing heavily.

"Hi," Reese whispered.

"Hi," she said back, her voice raspy and dry. She noticed soft sparks playing against his skin, and joy welled up in her heart. She wasn't broken after all, there was just something that'd been blocking them. Which raised the question of what.

"I take it that's my cue to leave then."

Both of them looked sharply towards where Penny was now standing. She was fidgeting uncomfortably, and her eyes were looking everywhere but the couple in front of her. Guilt consumed Faye. That wasn't very good behaviour on their parts. But being able to touch, being able to kiss, that was new. She'd have forgotten about the biggest night or day of her life when faced with that. She'd wanted to be able to touch her mate more than she wanted any other dream in her life. Including the dolls house she'd been desperate for as a child.

"No," Faye blurted out. She wasn't sure why, but the very idea of the woman leaving wasn't sitting right. In fact, it made her distinctly uneasy.

"Sorry, we've not been..." Reese started, looking down at his feet and shuffling about a bit. Faye placed a hand on his arm, almost pulling it back before remembering she could now. She didn't want him to feel bad about doing something they'd both wanted for so long.

"We haven't been able to touch until now." Faye finished for him.

"But I thought you said you'd been together since you were five?" Penny asked, looking straight at Reese. Faye frowned. Why had he told her that? It was true, but it could also have scared her off, which wasn't good in the slightest.

"We have," Reese said with a sigh.

"We could touch as kids, but never thought anything of it," Faye supplied. "The moment we turned eighteen, things changed. First for me, then for Reese a month later. It became painful to even brush hands. That's been our burden over since."

"But you've stayed together?" Penny frowned, an adorably confused look on her face.

"You're a paranormal too, I assume? You're not nearly freaked out enough by my light show just then not to be." Faye smiled slightly, amused by the twist in circumstances.

"Well, yes..."

"Could you leave your mate, if you wanted to?"

"Well, no, that's not how it works," she said.

"Exactly." Faye folded her arms, while retaking her seat at the table. "I couldn't leave Reese, even if I wanted to."

"Then what's changed? Did you use the potion?" This time, it was curiosity that lit up the red head's face. Faye found she liked that emotion even more.

"How do you know about that?" She frowned. She hadn't even told Reese about her sister's idea, never mind someone she'd only just met.

"Someone called Mia text, I didn't mean to read, but Reese was sending through the address, and I needed it, and..."

"It's fine, I'd have told him anyway. I just got distracted by the sudden need for catering." Faye laughed lightly.

"Sorry," Reese muttered. "But wait, what potion?"

"Mia made us a potion, she hoped it'd help with the no touching thing."

"Of course she did." He leaned back, smiling affectionately. Faye loved how close he was to her sisters. He always had been. As their next door neighbour growing up, and the four of them being fairly close in age, it'd made sense for him to know them well.

"But what changed?" Penny prompted, again.

"I have a theory," Faye said, thinking hard.

"Me too, but is there a way to test it?" Reese asked.

"You could kiss her too?" Faye teased, enjoying the slight shock on Penny's face. "Or I could call Ettie?"

"Ettie might be the easier option. She might slap me if we're wrong."

Faye laughed lightly. "I don't think we're wrong. My necklace opened earlier," she told him, then watched as delight, swiftly followed by confusion, washed over his face. It was kind of adorable how conflicted he was about it. Like he did and didn't want her to be his only mate.

"Try Ettie."

Faye nodded, picturing her familiar in her head. "Ettie," she whispered. She wasn't in the least bit surprised when a raven made up of bright white sparks appeared in front of them all, swooping about and trying to steal things from the dinner table. Silly bird. There was nothing there that could satisfy a bird made of magic there. Ettie couldn't even work.

"Impressive, but I'm not sure what I'm looking at," Penny said, her eyes not leaving Ettie as she flew about the room.

"How much do you know about witches and their familiars?" Faye asked.

"That they have them?"

Both Faye and Reese laughed.

"They are a little secretive. I've been mated to a witch for nearly twenty years, and even I still don't know much about them."

"Oi, you know as much as I do!" Faye protested indignantly.

"Which is..." Penny finally retook her seat, making Faye's heart soar. Good, they weren't going to lose her then.

"Familiars, like Ettie, appear to a witch when they turn eighteen. They're part of our magic, but seem to have a life of their own. But they never appear to anyone other than the witch they belong to. If they can belong. I'm sure Ettie would have a thing or two to say about belonging to anyone." Faye chuckled to herself.

"I hate to point this out, but I can see her as well as you can," Penny said.

"You can yes. There's only one other person a witch's familiar will appear to." Faye looked between Reese and Penny. "Well, in this case, two."

"And they are..."

"Mates," Faye said simply, watching the other woman's reaction closely.

7

HE WATCHED as the redhead's face witched from confused, to conflicted, to almost happy. But not quite. Though Reese suspected it was mostly the confusion that was making her react like that.

"What?" she blurted out. Reese exchanged a look with Faye, whose eyes had taken on a slightly nervous edge. He didn't really blame her, he was pretty much feeling exactly the same. Part of him was longing to go over to Penny and kiss her too, but then, he wasn't sure if that would be weird considering he'd just kissed Faye for the first time. He suspected that was the same kind of thing Faye was thinking. One of them needed to break the building tension, or something would explode and not in a good way.

"Mate, one, partner," he supplied.

"Or two." Faye smirked, already looking lighter now they'd touched. He felt that way too. It was surprisingly freeing compared to how they'd been feeling for most of their adult lines.

"How can anyone have two mates?" Penny asked, her eyes flitting between the two of them. Reese smiled. The way she was speaking wasn't as if she was someone that didn't believe. Quite the opposite. Her voice was filled with hope. Someone who thought what they were saying was right, but didn't want to commit in case they weren't.

"Easily," Faye answered. "We have a friend with three."

"Sounds like a lot of work," Penny muttered, making Reese laugh. He'd thought that too when Josh had told him about the set up he had with Eira. But then, if it was love, there wasn't much that could be done about it. That wasn't how paranormal mating worked. When someone like them met their mate, or their mates as the case may be, then that was it for them. The fact there'd been pain for him and Faye until Penny showed up, was almost enough of an indication as far as Reese was concerned.

"But this is different," Faye pointed out. This time, Reese frowned.

"How so?" he asked.

"With Eira, she has three mates, but each of them only has her. I think we're something different."

"What makes you say that?" He thought he knew where she was going, pretty much along the same lines he'd been thinking, but he wanted to be sure.

"Josh said there'd never been any pain for them. And my pain disappeared once I met Penny, but yours didn't..."

"...then went when I met her tonight." He nodded, pleased they were on the same line of thinking.

"But what does that mean?" Penny asked, confusion maring her pretty features.

"That if I kiss you, there'll be sparks," Faye answered, surprisingly serious.

"Oh." Penny swallowed visibly, and something tightened within Reese. He liked that idea. Almost as much as he liked the idea of kissing Penny himself. But then, it was probably a little bit creepier for him to make a move than Faye. Not that he'd ever been in this situation before. He glanced back at Faye. He'd never thought he'd ever be in a situation like this, either. But if it was the way he could be with Faye, then it was worth it for him.

"Is it okay if I try?" Faye asked softly, walking around so she was stood in front of the red head.

The women looked into each other's eyes, and it felt like they were in the room without him. It was that, more than anything, that convinced Reese this was the right thing for them all.

The air was already charged with magic. Whether it was from the sparks while he'd kissed Faye, the fact that the three of them were together for the first time, or the build up between the two of them.

"Yes," Penny whispered. Her voice was so quiet, that only his shifter hearing had been able to pick it up.

Slowly, Faye brushed a strand of hair behind Penny's ear, a small spark flying from her fingers as their skin touched. He could see her checking that Penny was alright with each and every moment. He only found it a little odd that Faye, who'd had her first ever kiss had been just moments before, taking charge of such an important moment. But there she was, beautiful and powerful, making the move that could seal things for them for life.

Her lips brushed against Penny's. Lightly, as if she was particularly worried. When the other woman didn't pull away, Faye seemed to gain courage, and deepened the kiss between them. Penny's hand tangled in Faye's hair. Sparks began to wash over the two of them. The white lights crackled around them, the brightest where they touched their bare skin.

Faye pulled Penny even closer with a hand around her waist. This time, the sparks jumped from the two women and onto Reese's own skin, dancing there like they had during his own kiss with Faye. He might have grown up around witches, but he wasn't entirely sure what it meant. Maybe this was the mating bond sealing for them? But then, it wasn't exactly like the scratching that was done by the bird shifters like him. Or the biting like the others. It wasn't even during sex.

Sex...that was actually a possibility now. No more hearing Faye's moans in the middle of the night when she thought he wasn't awake. He knew that was why she did it. He tried exactly the same when it all got too much. Now he'd be able to touch her. He'd be able to elicit those sounds himself. Or Penny would, while he watched. Maybe Penny could then join him. He guessed it was every man's fantasy. Two beautiful women. But he already knew that it was far more than that. If they said he could never watch, he'd be disappointed, but he'd go with it. If Penny said he could never touch her, he'd be equally as down about it, but he'd respect her wishes and leave her be.

So long as Faye was happy. So long as Penny was happy. So long as they were all happy.

Before him, the two women broke apart, and Penny's gaze flicked to his. She licked her lips, the glazed look on her face difficult to decipher. He hoped she wanted to kiss him too, but he didn't want to push it by bringing it up. He also didn't want to take advantage while she was already affected by Faye's magic. He knew first hand how much it could dull the senses.

"Faye," he warned. She nodded once, knowing him well enough to understand what his concern was. She stepped away, leaving the path clear between him and the other woman. He checked her face, surprised to see there wasn't even the slightest hint of jealousy there. Instead, there was a curiosity and a fulfillment that rivalled just about anything he'd ever witnessed before.

"Are you okay?" Faye asked her, lifting her hand to touch her face, before dropping it back to her side. She probably didn't want to freak Penny out. Though maybe it was just a reflex from when the two of them couldn't actually touch.

"I...I...I..." Penny stuttered, filling Reese with dread. She was going to run now, he was almost certain. He wasn't sure he even blamed her. It was a lot to take in.

"No one has to do anymore," Faye said softly, before pinning Reese with a look he didn't actually need, but acknowledged anyway.

"Whatever you're comfortable with," he added. But Penny's face didn't clear, she was still clearly uneasy by the situation. He hoped it was just a bit of shock and not them that'd done that.

"I...I...I don't know," she stammered. It was odd. She hadn't seemed like the nervous type before. But then again, he supposed he didn't really know her very well. Though he hoped that'd change soon.

None of them moved, and tension filled the air. There was definitely something brewing, and the urge to kiss her and seal what was between them, was tugging at the shifter inside Reese. It was already getting possessive, and there would be a point where he couldn't control it any longer.

Panic crossed the red head's face, and she turned, fleeing through their home and back out into the world. He just hoped they could find her again. Otherwise their mating would never be fulfilling.

8

SHE SHOULDN'T HAVE RUN. She was already feeling guilty for running. But the air had been so full of promise it'd been hard to ignore, and had she stayed...she dreaded to think what she'd have done. Well, not dreaded. She knew exactly what would have happened. And despite the concerns running around her head, it wouldn't have been too soon. It would have been just when it was supposed to be.

The only problem was that it scared her a little. The feeling, the promise, the seriousness. And she knew that would lead to conversations. Like what she was, how her kind mated. The real answer was that they didn't. Or they never had before. Her kind were made, not born. And by made, she meant cursed. None of them had any choice in being made into what they were. In fact, it even overrode their original DNA. It also made them forget what they'd been born as. Penny had often found herself wondering what she really was, but there was no point spending too much time dwelling on it. She'd never know. And she'd certainly never be able to get back what she was.

Now, the only thing she could hope for was that she never came across a dying child with the right combination of factors. So, basically, she just avoided children as much as she possibly could. It was the only way when she didn't know anymore about what the circumstances had to be for that to happen. Just another curse her kind seemed to bear.

Glancing at her watch, she cursed. Why was there so much time between now and when her yoga class was? At least while she was teaching, she didn't have to think about what'd just happened. As it stood, there were hours for her to dwell on the two people she'd left behind. And they were distracting her majorly. Seeing the two of them kiss had woken something within her she'd just assumed was dead. It wasn't desire. She'd felt that plenty of times. It was something more fundamental than that. It went bone deep.

She liked that. She hoped they did too. Which

just made her question *why* she'd run away. In that split second, it'd seemed like a great idea. Now she was out in the cold, not quite so much. But she couldn't go back now. Not without looking like the fool she was. They were probably laughing at her now, wondering what was wrong with her for running away from two such perfect people. They'd be right to. She was wondering what was wrong with her too.

"Penny?" a soft female voice called out into the night. One she recognised. Her heart skipped a beat. They'd come to look for her? No, that couldn't be possible. No one had ever come to look for her. At least, she didn't think they had. No one had attempted to ever tell her that they'd known her before she became...this. She'd only been a child then too. Surely she'd had parents who missed her? Apparently not.

"Here," she replied, not speaking above a whisper. She wasn't sure why. She wanted to be found. She thought, anyway. Being found meant that someone cared. Someone wanted her. But she didn't want to risk the rejection it would entail if she spoke louder and they *didn't* actually want her. Maybe she'd just forgotten something when she'd left.

"There you are," Faye sounded relieved, but

Penny still didn't turn around. She couldn't, not without risking letting the other woman see the tears in her eyes. Despite Penny's best efforts, Faye dipped around her so she was stood in front of her. "Hey, what's wrong?" Her voice was soft and caring, confusing Penny no end. No one had ever been like this with her. Faye leaned forward and wiped the tears from her cheeks.

"I'm sorry I freaked out," Penny muttered.

"Don't be sorry. It's completely understandable."

But why was this woman being so nice? Other than the fact she thought Penny was her mate. Though that was probably it. "But..."

"You don't know what you've given me already, Penny." Earnestness shone through Faye's eyes as she spoke, and Penny met her gaze, almost getting lost in the other woman's. "I couldn't even touch my mate until I met you. Well, one of my mates. But I've known Reese since I was five years old. Then when we were eighteen, and finally able to act on what we knew was between us, we couldn't. We tried to kiss once. It ended up in Reese staying away for a week. He only came back because it was too painful for his shifter side to be away from me for so long."

"It's true," Reese's voice rumbled, his hand touching the small of Penny's back. It was only a gentle touch, a tentative one to check she was okay with it, which she appreciated more than she could actually say. "Please don't put me through that again."

"Sorry?" Penny didn't think she understood. He was looking at her, not Faye, which implied he was talking to her and not the blonde. But that didn't make any sense. None at all. She couldn't make him feel like that.

"You should," Faye said to him softly. Reese nodded once.

He turned her ever so slightly so they were facing each other, and with an unrivalled tenderness, he leaned down and pressed his lips against hers. It took her a mere second to respond, even if she hadn't intended to. There was a tension in the air that was nothing like she'd ever experienced before. It filled her with anticipation, and with want. Pure, unadulterated want. She pressed her body against his, and he deepened their kiss, but kept it tender. It was so different from Faye's kiss before, and yet it held the same depth of potential emotion.

Disappointment engulfed Penny as the kiss ended, and she was left already yearning for more. He breathing was kind of laboured, and she knew both of them could tell how affected she was by them. The question was, did she really care? She glanced between the two of them, seeing the intense looks on their faces.

No. She didn't mind at all. Not if it led to two people like this in her life. She opened her mouth to speak, but was cut off by Faye holding up a hand.

"Don't say anything, we know it's a lot to take in, you can take all the time you want to think about it." She smiled softly, but Penny still caught her eyes glancing down to her lips.

"I know but-"

"How about a coffee?" Reese asked, his hand still pressed against Penny's back. She leaned back into his hand, appreciating the comfort he was giving her.

"Is there anywhere open at this time of night?" she asked, her voice shaking slightly.

"There's a little place, just down the street."

"That'd be good." A coffee sounded like a good plan. And being in public. She needed some time to process, even if she was sure about the two of them. Rushing into something, especially with two people who'd known each other for so long, sounded like a terrible idea.

9

FAYE WATCHED as Penny leaned back in her chair, seeming far more at ease now she had her hands around a steaming cup of coffee. Faye took a sip of her own, enjoying the bitter tones through the sweetness of the milk. She hadn't had a decent coffee in ages. Reese had bought a coffee machine a couple of months back in an attempt to make them, but he'd managed to break it accidentally. Much to her amusement. He could be a little clumsy like that.

Speaking of, Reese's eyes were flickering back and forth between her and Penny. She smiled to herself. The poor man really was confused. He was probably far more conflicted than she was. He liked to know exactly how things worked and why, having two mates was just going to be confusing for him.

And the fact that the second one was another woman...well if she knew Reese, then he was worrying that it meant he was being unfaithful to her. She had to admit it was a big leap from thinking she was the one for him for so long, to having to share. And be shared. But it was also something she looked forward to getting used to.

Though they may need to rearrange the beds. Then again, they'd need to do that anyway now she and Reese could touch. Staying in separate beds just didn't make sense anymore. Excitement rushed through Faye. It was only just hitting her that they'd now be able to experience the other side of their relationship. The one she'd only heard about from her sisters and pretended to know something about so she didn't end up looking like an innocent fool. Well, she was that anyway, and Mia had worked that out now. She wasn't sure whether Bex had, but not much slipped past her eldest sister. Sometimes, Faye even thought she was too intelligent for her own good. It took a certain level of thinking to be able to hide a child for as long as Bex had.

At least they knew about Fiona now. Though not who her father was. It didn't really make any sense. Paranormals *couldn't* have children with anyone that wasn't their mate. That just wasn't how it worked.

But Bex also wasn't mated. Or she wasn't as far as Faye knew. So they had no idea *who* Fiona's father was, or how she'd come about. And there was never really a good time to bring it up. Now that the family knew about the little girl, she went everywhere with Bex. It was like they were making up for lost time.

"Faye? Are you okay?" Reese asked, resting a hand on her leg. Her heart skipped a beat at the small touch, and because of the affection it conveyed. This was what they'd been missing in their relationship. What she was glad to finally have with him. She glanced at Penny. What she hoped to have with them both.

"Sorry, I was thinking about my family."

Reese smiled at her affectionately. It was one of the many things she loved about him. He thought of her family as if they were his own. And she supposed they were.

"What are they like?" Penny asked softly.

"Intrusive. But they love me. They love us all." Faye smiled to herself. "I'm the youngest of three, so my parents doted on me a little as a child. It sent my middle sister, Mia, up the wall. Especially when our eldest joined in."

"You're one of three then?"

"Yes, and Bex has a little girl now."

Penny frowned and Penny longed to know what she was thinking of. "Do you want children?" she asked.

"Some day." Faye shrugged. "But up until now, we've had bigger things to worry about. Plus, neither of my sisters were mated, so there weren't really any children about to make me want any."

"Makes sense," Penny muttered and looked away. Faye exchanged a worried glance with Reese. There was clearly something more going on, but she didn't want to pry. At least, not yet. One day she'd discover what was wrong with the other woman, and why the talk of children was making her so uncomfortable. Even if she had been the one to bring it up.

"What about you? Any desire for children?" She regretted her question almost the moment she asked as she watched hurt flash across Penny's face.

"It's not really an option for me."

"Maybe now it is," Faye responded, reaching out for the hand Penny was resting against the table. She placed hers around it, enjoying the feel of skin against skin, and hoping it offered the red head the comfort she needed.

"Not of my own," she muttered. Faye's heart sank. That didn't sound good. She wondered if there was anything any of them could do. Maybe

Mia could sort out some kind of potion if not, it was what she was best at after all. Penny stared into her now empty coffee mug, looking a bit morose.

"Want to see a trick?" Reese asked suddenly, boyish glee lighting up his face.

"Not here," Faye hissed, already worried about what he might be up to. Knowing him, it'd be something like shifting and stealing a part of the plant that seemed to be perched above the counter of the shop.

"I wasn't going to do that." He pouted slightly. Clearly she wasn't the only one feeling a lot lighter for their change in circumstances. Now all the had to do was cheer Penny up, and then see where the night took them. Hopefully to a lot of laughter and joy. Seemed they could all deal with that.

"No." Penny sat back properly, a haunted look in her eyes. "No, no, no, no, no."

"What's wrong?" Faye leaned forward, anxious to make whatever it was better for the other woman.

"Run, run, run, run."

"We're not going anywhere," Reese assured her.

"You should," she replied, looking like she was desperately trying to hold something back, though what that something was, was still a complete mystery. Faye'd never seen anyone look like that before.

Penny's head tipped back, and her face stretched, turning darker and far more menacing. But neither of them flinched away. There was something deep within Faye assuring her that Penny was still her mate, and she wasn't in any danger from her, even if she did look like a completely different person.

It wasn't until an ear piercing scream filled the café, that the pieces slot together for her, and she realised what Penny was.

The only confusion lay in that Faye hadn't realised banshees existed.

10

HE CRADLED Penny to his chest, feeling her shivering against him. Her teeth began to chatter. He hated it. Seeing her so vulnerable was physically painful. He was vaguely aware of Faye spinning a tale about allergies to the other people in the cafe,. He was just grateful they hadn't seemed to hear her scream. Well, other than the vampire in the corner. But he scarpered off quickly afterwards. Ridiculous, if anyone asked Reese. Just because beings liked banshees existed, it didn't mean the legends about them were true.

"What are you still doing here?" she asked weakly.

"You didn't think we'd abandon you, did you?" He stroked her cheek, before pushing a stray strand of hair behind her ear. Her eyes looked up at him, grateful and in awe.

"You should have done, its not safe to be near me right now. Or ever." She shuddered and looked away.

"Nothing to see, she just forgot she can't eat cinnamon. She does it all the time," Faye told a few more bystanders. She turned towards the two of them. "You think we care you're a banshee?" she demanded.

"You should." Her voice cracked, making the tears she was trying to conceal all the more obvious.

Faye sunk to her knees, reaching out to turn Penny's face upwards so their gazes locked.

"We don't. You're ours. We're yours. It doesn't matter what you are. Just like it doesn't matter that Reese can turn into a raven, or I can make sparks appear. How we're born doesn't define who we are. It's what we do with our lives that counts." She sat back on her heels, looking pretty pleased with her little speech. Penny didn't look so sure.

"But I wasn't born this way," she whispered hesitantly.

"Banshees aren't born?" he asked, receiving a shake of her head in return. "No wonder you're so rare." He'd almost thought they were a myth himself. Until one had started screaming right in front of him. That was a pretty good reason to start believing.

"No, we're made."

"Like vampires?" Faye asked, a frown covering her face. He wouldn't admit it aloud, but he'd been wondering the same thing.

"No. At least, I don't think so. I don't actually know beyond the banshee curse can only be passed to a paranormal child. And that it stops them being who they were. I always thought it would erase their mate too, but..."

"But here we are." Faye's frown transformed into a broad grin, lighting up her face. He imagined his own probably mirrored up.

"Yes. But..."

"But?" Faye prompted after a moment's silence.

"I'm still a harbinger of death," she pointed out.

"I thought banshees only warned?" he said softly.

"We do..."

"Hardly a harbinger then." He smiled down at her, and for the first time since she'd collapsed, she returned it

"Are you two really okay with this? I know nothing about how my powers work. I can't answer your questions. Probably ever."

"Then we'll figure it out together," Faye reassured

her. "I might even know someone who can tell us more."

"You do?" Hope lit up Penny's voice.

"Possibly. We can agree that you have death magic, not light magic. Right?"

Reese tried not to laugh. Faye only ever used 'right' as a question when she already knew she was right.

"I guess so, but I can't say I've ever thought about it." Penny sat up suddenly, and Reese mourned the loss of contact. At the same time, he knew it was for the best. While they'd been having their conversation quietly, it still wasn't the place.

"It makes sense," he admitted, trying to ignore the smug look on his blonde mate's face.

"I know," Faye responded. She stood up and held out her hand for Penny, helping the other woman to her feet. Reese followed swiftly, jumping up with a grace only a bird shifter could claim. He cracked his neck. Shifting soon was probably a good idea. It'd been a while, and he was starting to suffer the itch of his inner raven trying to get out.

Maybe he should fly to wherever Faye intended them to go. His sense of direction was unparalleled, and his shifter form was only slightly larger than a normal raven, so it wasn't like he'd be spotted and raise any suspicions.

He caught Faye's eye and she nodded once. Years of knowing his shifting patterns, and years of knowing him, meant she didn't need words.

"Yes. We're off to see Isabella," Faye responded, causing Reese to groan. He knew the necromancer from high school, and they'd never really got on. "Oh, don't look at me like that, Reese. She's grown up since school."

He raised an eyebrow.

"Alright, maybe not. But she's the best shot we have since Damien went rogue."

"I'd hardly call what he's doing 'going rogue', Faye." Or at least, it wasn't in Reese's book. After the Necromancer Council had been suspended, an odd sort of martial law had come into effect for them. Damien's part in that was to chase down the kind of necromancers who'd caused the issue in the first place. In other words, the ones who killed people. Or reanimated the unwilling dead. Although, how the dead could be willing was another matter.

"The point is moot." She waved her hand to dismiss the conversation. "Isabella is our chance for answers."

"True..."

"I feel like I'm missing something," Penny muttered.

"We're off to see a necromancer," Faye answered sweetly.

"An immature necromancer," he muttered.

"Reese!" Faye admonished. She turned so she was just facing Penny. "She's really not that bad. Most of the time anyway."

Reese's shifter hearing picked up Penny's gulp. He felt for her. She had no idea what she was in for.

11

PENNY LOOKED at the surprisingly plain front door, and frowned. It wasn't what she'd expected when the other two had started on about a necromancer. She'd been expecting dark and dingy. Maybe with a haunted house vibe. Certainly animal skeletons littering the garden. Instead, she got nothing more than a white picket fence.

"Are we in the right place?" Her voice shook as she asked.

"Yes. Isabella's family has lived here since we were at school." Faye looked up at the sky, and Penny followed her gaze, spotting a speck of black getting ever closer to them. "Ah, here he is."

"Is that...?"

"In the feather," Faye replied with a light laugh.

The bird landed on Faye's shoulder and cocked its head.

"Hi, Reese," Penny said, feeling a little silly talking to a bird, even if the bird was part of her mate. One of her mates.

Reese chirped at her, assumably in greeting, before turning to Faye and making a series of sounds she could only describe as irritated.

"No, Reese. I left your clothes at the café because I thought sending you to meet Isabella completely naked. Although...the plan does have some merits. What do you reckon, Penny?" A smirk played at the corner of Faye's mouth.

To Penny's surprise, she had to smother a laugh. "I think it's a great idea." The words slipped out before she realised what she was saying. Faye's part-smirk turned into a beaming smile.

"Here, you daft bird." She handed him a small bag, which he grasped in his beak, before flapping off and into a dark secluded space.

Disappointment that he'd actually be fully dressed surprised Penny. That wasn't normally her reaction to anyone.

Reese appeared moments later, his hair looking slightly ruffled. He strode up to Penny and kissed her gently on the lips. He pulled away, and repeated the action with Faye. It was the first time she'd seen them kiss since accepting they were her mates, and she was only a little surprised at the lack of jealousy within her. Even more so by how she was already feeling less like the two of them were a couple with her on the outside. She knew that would've sunk in with time, but she hadn't expected it quite so soon.

"I thought about not kissing you in punishment..." he started, his eyes a lot softer than his words implied they'd be.

"But that's too cruel," Faye finished for him, her face lighting up in a smile.

"It would be yes. We've had too much time wasted for us."

"Sorry," Penny muttered.

"No!" Faye's instant reply came. "Never be sorry for something outside your control. There's a reason we've met when we have, and that doesn't have anything to do with it being your fault."

Penny stood there for a moment, stunned. She wasn't sure what to make of it. Part of her still felt guilty for not being around sooner, even if that was a ridiculous thing to think. It wasn't her fault, just like it wasn't Reese or Faye's faults either. All it was, was bad luck.

"Okay," she muttered softly.

"Good, now let's go see Isabella," she said, striding the remaining few paces between them and the door, and rapping her knuckles against it firmly. Penny hurried so she was standing behind her, with an uneasy looking Reese next to her. He really wasn't a fan of this Isabella person then. She wondered what had gone on between them for him to be so uneasy. But that was a question for another day. It probably wasn't best to ask for the down low on the person they hoped would give them answers.

"Hello?" a sleepy voice said from the door. Ah, at least Isabella *looked* like what Penny expected of a necromancer. She had pale skin, with long dark hair and bright eyes that seemed to swirl with colour. There was also something a little off about her, but she couldn't put her finger on what. Maybe it was just the banshee reaction to her necromancer magic. The two couldn't mix well given necromancers could interrupt the banshee warning system by simply bringing the dead back to life.

Not that she imagined it would be simple. She knew nothing about necromancers, and didn't want to cast any aspersions without knowing the truth about them.

"Isabella!" Faye chirped, sticking her hand on the door frame so the other woman wouldn't close it on them. Well, she could still close it on them, but it'd be terribly rude, even if they were their uninvited.

"I see you brought bird brain." Isabella narrowed her eyes at Reese, who made a weird, almost part growling noise. Faye held a hand out behind her, trying to touch him and likely ground him, but failing. Instead, Penny placed her hand on his arm, and squeezed gently. He looked in her direction, and his expression softened, leaving the path clear for the Reese she'd come to know.

"Good evening, Isabella," he said through gritted teeth. Pride welled up in Penny. She hoped he'd always be so reasonable.

"We need some help," Faye said, ignoring Reese. Probably for the best, Penny wasn't too sure how much longer he could actually stay quiet.

"Of course you do," Isabella snarled. "Why else would you be here?" Okay, so she clearly wasn't happy about this. And that wasn't helping with how nervous Penny was feeling about the whole situation.

"We just have some questions about death magic. Our mate, Penny...."

"What?" Isabella demanded, her eyes meeting Penny's and turning into a death glare that could only be rivaled by one from the devil himself. "Why have you brought *that* here?" she spat out. Penny swallowed loudly. This wasn't good at all.

"She's our mate."

"Shut up, Faye," Isabella growled. Then, with a surprising amount of speed and grace given she'd just appeared to wake up, Penny found herself pinned against the wall of the house. She was facing in the opposite direction with a hand around her neck, and angry eyes boring into her. "Why are you here?" Isabella demanded.

"A-a-answers," she stuttered out, her words inhibited by her windpipe being crushed. That was inconvenient to say the least.

"And you think I'll give them to a banshee?" The venom in her voice wasn't like anything Penny had ever heard. She wondered if the problem was between Isabella and banshees, or necromancers and banshees, but she imagined she'd find out fairly soon.

"Enough, Isabella," Reese growled, pulling the hand away from Penny's neck. She gasped in relief, sucking in deep gulps of air in an attempt to regain her composure.

"How *dare* you bring her here!" Isabella kicked and tried to scratch at Reese's face.

"Why?" Faye asked softly.

"Do you seriously not know?" The shock seemed to stop the dark-haired woman's attack, and Reese let go of her.

"No, that's why we're asking." Penny could hear the lack of patience in Faye's voice, but, thankfully, the other two hadn't caught on. Reese caught her eye. Okay then, just Isabella hadn't caught on.

"Fine. But only cause I want her gone. Maybe when you understand why, you'll do something about her." The menace was plain, but at least she knew two people had her back. "Better come in then."

Isabella's glare was really getting on Faye's nerves. There was no real need for it. She'd never met Penny before, and even if she had, Faye was sure that Penny had never done anything to hurt the necromancer, that just wasn't part of her inherent nature. She knew she shouldn't feel like that already, after all, she barely knew the other woman, but there was still something about her that made Faye so certain.

"What are you after, Faye?" Isabella broke the silence with a snarl.

"We need to know about death magic."

"And what makes you think I'll tell you and bird brain about that?"

Faye scowled. She knew Isabella and Reese hadn't got on in school, though she'd never known *why* that was. However, she had thought that the two of them would have moved on from whatever the disagreement was. The scowl on Reese's face, and Isabella's entire demeanor, suggested otherwise though.

"Please, Isabella. We know nothing, and Penny screamed earlier. We need to properly know what it's about."

"And you think I know?"

"Yes. We're all more than aware you father sat on the Council before it was disbanded. I highly doubt you don't," Faye pointed out. She'd always found Isabella's father a little intimidating. He was like an older, male version of his daughter. The stereotypical image of a vampire more than a necromancer, though that was mostly because most humans seemed oblivious to the existence of necromancers, despite the fact they were far more dangerous than vampires, who tended towards just being a bit bitey really. They weren't about to kill anyone for their life essence.

"Fine. I know things." Isabella sighed. That was easier than Faye had expected.

"Why were you so angry we'd brought Penny?" she asked. It might not be the most important thing they needed to ask, but it was still something they needed to know. Especially if it meant they had to try and stay away from necromancers in general. Though that could prove pretty difficult considering most paranormals led every day lives. The woman at the coffee shop could be a fae, or the cleaner for next door's house could be a wolf shifter. She wasn't, but the point was still valid.

"You really don't know a thing about banshees, do you?" Isabella asked, a resigned tone in her voice.

"No, that's why we're asking," Reese griped.

"Reese!"

"Sorry," he muttered. Faye hoped that'd be the last of him interrupting. He really wasn't going to help the situation.

Isabella let out a raucous laugh. "I see how it is. Someone finally tamed the bird."

"She's had me tamed for years, and you know it," Reese responded instantly. Faye threw him a dirty look, but he just shrugged.

"I still say you had until you turned eighteen." Isabella waggled her eyebrows and her meaning finally sunk in. Sparks ignited on Faye's hands, and it was all she could do to keep them in check. Even once she'd extinguished them, she could still feel the power crackling beneath her finger tips. She was going to have to be careful, or she'd end up with a bigger problem on her hands. She was sure she could feel more power than she'd ever felt before. Apparently, meeting Penny had been good for more than just being able to touch Reese. She'd have to try some bigger magic at some point. Maybe she could get Bex to teach her.

"Moving on. Banshees," she prompted.

The tension from Penny, who was sat next to her on the worn sofa, was almost touchable, and without meaning to, she took her hand in her own, giving it a squeeze. Penny returned it, and contentment flowed through Faye. This was what mating was supposed to be like.

"They're necromancers."

"What?" Penny blurted out.

"Well, they're not. But they used to be." Isabella examined one of her nails, as if she hadn't just dropped a major bombshell on them all.

"You mean..."

"Before they're given the banshee curse, yes."

"How does that work?" Faye asked, curious, but also knowing she wanted to know for other reasons. She didn't think Penny would agree to children until she knew how the curse worked. Not from her reaction to talk of kids earlier. And while Faye didn't want them now, she did at some point. Hopefully the fact neither her, nor Reese, had any death magic, would help with the situation.

"It's to do with the banshee scream." Isabella shrugged. "We don't know the specifics, but if a necromancer child hears a banshee scream at an exact age, we're talking down to the minute, they become cursed. No one is sure what happens after that, other than that the children disappear." She seemed very unaffected to be talking about missing children, but that could just be her immaturity coming through. Isabella had always been a little bit that way. It was one of the reasons Faye had never been closer to her.

"So I could curse someone without meaning to?" Penny asked, horror filling her voice.

"Yes. And steal our family from us," Isabella snapped. Which was when it all clicked into place for Faye.

"You lost a sibling, didn't you?" she asked softly.

"Yes, our middle sister. She was only five when it happened. It was awful, the sound shook my very soul. But it did far, far, worse to her." Tears pooled in the woman's eyes, and for the first time, Faye felt kind of sorry for her. Though it didn't stop the slightly jealous monster simmering beneath the surface, nor the anger over how Isabella had treated Penny when they'd first arrived.

"I'm sorry."

"Don't be. It's not *your* fault. But that's why banshees are so rare. The circumstances are so specific, and a lot of necromancers just keep their children inside between the ages of four and five. If they can, and if they know, anyway." She looked away, and Faye wondered what else there was to it.

"Oh."

"Yes, oh."

"Do you know what the scream means?"

"Other than the loss of a child?" Isabella laughed bitterly. "Normally it's a warning that something bad is coming. Sometimes death, sometimes just pain and anguish. At least, as far as we can tell, that's what they're about. But there's still not enough information for us to go on. You're on your own for that one, I'm afraid."

"Is that seriously all you can tell us?" Reese spat.

"Yes. Though it appears she has some life magic now, probably her connection between the two of you," Isabella said, her tone softening properly for the first time.

"How can you tell that?" Faye asked. Life and death magic were still shrouded in mystery for her, as they were for most paranormals. She suspected the only ones who had any clue were the necromancers themselves. Everyone else just seemed to know they had life magic, and that was it.

"Necromancers can see mating bonds. Didn't you know that?" Isabella cocked her head to the side as if asking why they wouldn't.

"No. That's not common knowledge." Faye's anger rose as she realised Isabella had probably been able to see the link between her and Reese even when they'd been at school. Meaning hitting on him had been a really low blow on her part. She just about managed to keep her anger under control though. Which was definitely a good thing. Exploding here wouldn't be a good idea. Well, exploding anywhere wouldn't be.

"Oh. Well, we can. The one between you and bird brain is pretty strong, but a little twisted. As if you've sealed it wrong." Isabella's brows furrowed. Faye opened her mouth to try and head her off so she didn't question what was going on too much. She didn't want anyone else knowing about their odd predicament. Isabella held up her hand to stop her from speaking. "It's got a slight kink in it that suggests it was more twisted before, so whatever it is you're doing now, is working. Then there's another bond between each of you and the banshee. That one's faint, but it's been growing stronger by the second." She frowned.

"That's good then." Faye smiled, hoping that was enough to satisfy the necromancer's curiosity. Though she doubted it.

"I've heard triad mating are rare. Treasure it," she said sadly, surprising Faye. She hadn't expected that response from the woman.

"You'll find your someone," Reese said, surprisingly calmly given how much he seemed to dislike the woman.

"Maybe. Or maybe it's just not in the cards for me."

"Give it time," Faye responded.

"Is that all?" The necromancer rose to her feet, straightening out her skirt. That was a dismissal if ever Faye had heard one.

"Yes, thank you Isabella, I know you didn't have to..."

"If it stops another child from being cursed by her knowing, then it's worth it. I suppose." She shrugged, but the pain in her eyes was evident.

"I hope it does. And maybe we can find your sister?" Faye suggested.

"I doubt it."

"What's her name?" Penny asked, speaking up for the first time in a while. Faye grasped her hand tighter.

"Carmen."

"If we find her, we'll make sure she comes back to you," she promised softly.

Isabella just nodded. "Thank you."

13

"BEX, Bex, please. Calm down and talk slower," Faye asked as she paced back and forth in front of him. He was worried already. Bex was fiercely independent, probably even more so since her fake wedding and secret child. Well, the wedding had been real. And the marriage. But the reasons behind it hadn't been, and as far as Reese was aware, there was barely any contact between Bex and Robert now that his part of the disaster at the wedding had come out.

He strained his ears, trying to hear the other part of the conversation, but it seemed like Bex was a little too worked up for that. It was a miracle Faye could tell what she was saying. Maybe it was a woman thing.

"What's happening?" Penny asked, placing a

gentle hand on his arm. He found it oddly soothing, and wished she'd do it more.

"I'm not too sure. Faye'll tell us in a moment," he said with a frown. Faye was now waving her spare hand around, talking animatedly. Maybe he needed to get Mia involved too. But no, that wasn't a good idea until after he'd spoken to Faye.

"Who's she talking to?"

"Her oldest sister. I hope nothing's wrong with her daughter."

"She's not a..."

"No, I don't think so. Bex is a witch. But none of us know who her daughter's father is."

"So she could be part necromancer?" Penny sounded nervous, and he turned so he could put his arm around her, pulling her close. She nuzzled into his chest, and something uncoiled inside him. He hadn't realised quite how worried he'd been about her not actually wanting to have anything with him. He'd have respected that, naturally, but he'd have been sad.

"I suppose so, yes. But it seems a little unlikely."

"Keep me away from her," she begged, her emotional eyes up at him filled with her plea.

"Faye'll be sad if you don't want to meet her," he pointed out.

"It's not safe," she protested weakly. So she did have a soft spot for children. That was good to know. It meant he had a chance of them in the future, though how that was going to work was a little beyond him. He supposed the child would be his and Faye's, at least biologically. He had no doubt Penny would be as much of a parent to whatever offspring they had.

"I'm sure it will be. Fiona isn't even five yet. You've got months to meet her with it being perfectly safe." He brushed a strand of hair out of her eyes. She was beautiful. Not the same kind of beautiful as Faye, but equally so.

"Oh, I suppose then. But then I won't be able to see her for a year." Tears began to pool in Penny's eyes, and his heart broke for her. He was under the impression she'd been alone far longer than anyone should have been. At least he and Faye could change that now.

"We'll explain it to her. What about if you talked on the phone? If you wanted to I mean. You can tell when you're going to scream, right?"

"Yes."

He nodded. He'd thought that was what her repeated use of the word no was earlier, but wanted to be sure. "We could do that, then you can hang up the phone when you feel one coming. Or maybe one of us can always be there and do something about it if we think something is about to go wrong."

"You'd do that for me?" she asked in awe.

"Of course we would," Faye answered, touching her hand to the other woman's back, before trailing it down so her skin touched his as well as their shared mate. "We're a team, Penny, and that means we support you whatever you need. And Bex will understand. Not right this second, but she'll understand when we tell her." She leaned forward and pressed a kiss to the top of Penny's head. There was something about this situation, as unusual as it seemed, that felt right.

He pulled Penny in closer, and opened his other arm to Faye, who snuggled herself into him too. This was heaven. Having the two of them so connected to him was what he'd been missing his entire life.

"What was wrong with Bex?"

"They've found something." Faye frowned.

"What kind of something?"

"A prison, I think."

"She shouldn't even be looking." He felt the anger rising inside him. He'd thought Bex was leaving the whole situation well alone. But apparently not.

"I know. But I think Robert found it, then told

her. What else was she to do, I guess?" She looked unsure, but he knew she had a point.

"Robert shouldn't be looking either. He could get himself hurt," Reese protested. Plus, he didn't trust Robert in the slightest. Even ignoring the fact he let himself be controlled by a group of witch hunters, there was something iffy about him. Reese had never liked him, even when he'd just been Bex's plus one.

"He's probably trying to redeem himself," Faye muttered.

"For what?" Penny looked between the two of them, an adorably confused look on her face.

"Marrying my sister because they were being blackmailed, causing my niece to get kidnapped, causing my other sister to get kidnapped, ruining Bex's wedding. Take your pick." Faye shrugged.

"I hardly think ruining Bex's wedding is a real option there, Bex knew what she was doing, and Robert was fake marrying her from the start," Reese pointed out. He knew that Bex had been under alot of stress, particularly with poor Fiona missing, but there was a part of him that thought she was at least a little to blame. Or that she at least wasn't blame-less. If she'd *told* her family about her four year old daughter, then there would have been less danger in the poor thing being kidnapped, and more people to help find her.

Then again, he could understand why she didn't. Being unmated, and having a child, was unheard of. Not even just rare. It really shouldn't happen. And there were still a lot of unanswered questions for Bex. He had even more questions now. If Penny couldn't have children, but wanted to, then there was a chance that Bex may know of a way to make it so she could have one. That would be worth the awkward conversation.

"It is too. He still brought the witch hunters. He still brought Mia to their attention and got her drugged." Faye shrugged out from under his arm, and crossed her arms across her chest. He was in trouble then.

"Well yes..."

"So he has plenty to make up for," Faye pointed out, pouting slightly.

"It sounds like she has a point," Penny pointed out.

"Huh, is this what I'm going to have to live with now? Being ganged up on all the time?" He laughed despite himself. They were kind of cute when they were both angry at him. Not that he was going to tell them that, it'd probably just end with them yelling at him.

"Maybe." Faye smirked, clearly amused with his reaction.

"I look forward to it."

Penny laughed, completely at ease for the first time since he'd met her. He leaned down, and kissed her lips gently. When he pulled away, she pressed her fingers to her lips. "What was that for?" she asked, seeming so innocent, it hurt.

"You're my mate, do I need a reason?"

"No, I suppose not. But..." She glanced off towards Faye, who'd relaxed a little and was looking on with a smile on her face that stretched all the way to her eyes.

"You're both our mates, Penny. The bond isn't designed for jealousy. How do you feel when I kiss Reese?"

He watched Penny's reaction carefully, wondering what she'd do. When she turned a delightful shade of pink, pride welled up within him. Yes, she did have a definite innocence about her. He wondered just how far it went. Then again, he supposed it didn't really matter. It wasn't like he and Faye had any experience either. That was the problem with being mated but unable to touch.

"I like it," she whispered.

"Good," he responded, before kissing her again.

"But what do we do now?" she asked once they'd parted, looking between him and Faye.

"We're waiting on Bex finding out more, but I think we're going to need to go find the place she's on about."

"Yeah, I think so too," he agreed. That was one of the problems with being a witch. For some reason, their policing system sucked. Probably because the Council wanted to be as peaceful as possible. Which he understood, but sometimes, it really wasn't practical. Like now. If they told the Council about the witch hunters, all that would happen was they'd debate it for ages before doing anything about it. If they did anything at all. It didn't matter that the hunters had been after them for centuries.

As long as there were witches, there'd be people hunting them, he guessed.

"Which means what?" Penny asked.

"We can go home and rest for a bit." Faye gave Reese a knowing look, and he nodded. They'd waited for too long not to do what they wanted to now they had a little bit of time.

"Okay, can you drop me off at mine on the way? I've no idea where we are?" A disappointed expression crossed her face. She'd misunderstood Faye's intentions then.

"You can come with us," he told her, watching first delight, and then wariness passing over her features.

"I don't want to impose."

Faye moved back in closer, so she was just a hair's breadth away from Penny's face. She reached out a hand and brushed the other woman's cheek. "We want you to come back with us," she whispered.

Reese slowly removed him arm from around Penny, allowing Faye the access she wanted. She slid her arm around the redhead's waist, and pulled her in close, before pressing her body against her, and letting their mouths join in a slow, drawn out kiss.

14

PENNY WAS NERVOUS. It wasn't like she hadn't done this before, but she didn't want to slip up and make either of the other two nervous. Because it was clear, both from the glances they were throwing each other, and from the things they'd been saying about the situation, that they *hadn't*. Which meant they were probably relying a little on her to direct things, even if they didn't realise that's what they were doing.

After a few moments of the three of them just stood there, she strode forward and pressed her lips against Faye's. It took the blonde a moment to respond, but soon her tongue was tangling with Penny's. Faye groaned, and pressed her body more firmly against her. Penny slipped her hand around her waist. She slipped her other hand under the bottom of Faye's shirt, touching the smooth skin there, and making the other woman shiver. She was clearly sensitive, which could only make this more fun for them all.

Penny broke away from Faye, and looked around the room, focusing on it for the first time. She'd been too focused on the two people in it before hand. Her heart broke when she noticed the two beds, both about three quarter sized. She wondered just how long her mates had been torturing themselves for. Probably as long as they'd been together. She hated that, but at least she could make it better.

"Do you think we could push the beds together?" she asked, a little breathlessly. There was no way the three of them were going to all fit in one that size.

"Yes," Reese said, moving over to the one of the left.

"Reese?" Faye asked in a small voice.

"Hmm?"

"Do you mind if I try?" She nodded at her hands which were already glowing a pale white with the sparks that were there. Penny thought back to how they'd felt against her skin during their first kiss, and couldn't wait to feel them again. It'd been unlike anything she'd ever experienced before. But then again, kissing Faye, and Reese, had been nothing like she'd ever expected either.

"Go ahead," he said, his eyes lighting up with pride as he stepped back, motioning for Penny to do the same.

A look of severe concentration crossed Faye's face, and sparks jumped from her hands towards the two beds. Nothing happened for a moment, but then, with a shake and a shudder, they moved together. The meeting of the two beds was a little rough. And the made a thumping sound, but other than that, it seemed to work perfectly, and the two beds were finally side by side.

"I did it!" Faye sounded far more delighted than she possibly should given that she'd just performed magic. As far as Penny knew, she was a witch. And the whole point of witches was that they could do magic of one sort or another. Or at least, she thought it was. If not, then she had a lot of reevaluating to do.

"You did." Reese beamed as he looked on. The mood slightly altered with Faye's magic.

"I don't have to hide it anymore."

"No, you don't." Penny could hear the affection in Reese's voice. Affection that was reflected in her own feelings, though she couldn't for the life of her explain why she was feeling them. Other than that

Faye was happy, and her happiness meant the world to Penny. It hit her that she was no longer alone in the world. And that she never had to be alone in the world ever again. It was an odd revelation, but one she very much liked the sound of.

"Did what? Magic?" she asked for clarification.

"Yes," Faye responded, a giddy look on her face. "Big magic." She beamed.

"What she means to say, is that she's never managed to do anything that big before. She's been trying for years, but nothing seems to have worked. So now..."

"Now you've come along," Faye finished, bouncing over to Penny and pulling her close, kissing her far more firmly and passionately that Penny had expected.

Slowly, Faye walked backwards, pulling Penny with her until the two of them hit the bed. Without breaking the kiss, Faye lay back on the bed, and Penny found herself straddling the other woman, still kissing her. They were close, but not quite as close as Penny would have liked. There were too many clothes for that.

She broke the kiss and sat up, lifting the edge of her shirt and beginning to pull it over her head.

Beneath her, Faye shook her head. "Let me," she whispered huskily.

Penny cocked her head to the side, not too sure what Faye had in mind. Or at least, she didn't until the sparks lit up Faye's hands again. This time, they danced over their clothing, and awareness dawned on her, as the clothes vanished, landing in a crumpled heap on the floor.

"Damn it," Faye muttered.

"Why? It worked didn't it?" Penny asked, admiring the swell of Faye's now naked breasts and the stretch of skin that made up her stomach. Maybe if she moved backwards slightly, they'd be able to see even more. But all in good time.

"They're supposed to be folded." She pouted, which was just an invitation to kiss her. Penny leaned down and tugged Faye's lips between her teeth gently, making the other woman groan and buck against her. Good. That was exactly the reaction she wanted. The only problem was, she didn't want Faye squirming out of the way when she touched her more.

"Reese?" she asked.

"Yes, Penny," he responded, moving over to the bed and perching on the side of it. There was a hooded look in his eyes that told her he was as affected by the situation as they were, and he hadn't even been touched yet. Then again, the tension was a palpable thing, creating an intense atmosphere in the room that would have affected a nun.

"Can you hold Faye's arms for me?" she asked, watching the pair of them closely to check they were okay with it. Interest flared in both of their eyes, and Reese nodded, moving around so he could do as she asked. He leaned down and kissed Faye once, it was chaste, and more to show trust and affection than anything else.

"You okay?" Penny asked, and Faye nodded in return. "Good."

She swung her leg over so she was perched next to Faye, then trailed her hand up one of her legs, enjoying the soft whimpers that slipped from the other woman's lips.

She moved her hand inwards, Faye's legs involuntarily falling open, allowing Penny to tease between them, causing more whimpers to fall from her lips. Slowly, and making sure Faye was comfortable the whole time, she slipped one of her fingers inside her, curling upwards. Faye's hips bucked off the bed, and she moaned loudly.

Reese still held onto her arms, watching them intently, but not doing anymore. Penny liked that.

She appreciated the respect he was giving to their time. Besides, he knew he'd get him.

Penny pushed Faye's legs further apart so she could move between them. The blonde looked down her body, meeting Penny's eyes, so she gave her a wicked grin before lowering her mouth between her legs, drawing her tongue along Faye's entrance. The whimpers increased, as did the pace at which Penny moved her fingers. She could tell from the shuddering of the woman beneath her, that Faye wasn't going to last much longer.

"Please," Faye begged, though Penny wasn't all that sure she was aware of what she was saying. Satisfaction filled her. *She* was doing this to her. No one else. Just her.

Sparks emerged along Faye's skin, moving themselves swiftly onto Penny's own, and she was sure onto Reese's too. She felt Faye's legs stiffen, and the long drawn out scream that followed was accompanied by a flash of light as Faye's sparks exploded along with her.

15

A LOUD BUZZING woke Reese from his sleep, and it took him a few minutes to realise one of their phones was going off. A heavy weight was pressed against his arm, and he looked across to find Faye wrapped around Penny, who was nestled against him. He smiled lazily at the sleeping women. At his sleeping mates. No one could doubt that's what they were now. After Faye had filled the room with white light, he'd marked them too. And though the scratch marks wouldn't be visible to anyone, any shifter would be able to sense them. He suspected some other paranormals could also sense the marks, but he had no proof of that.

The buzzing continued, and he remembered what had woken him. He twisted around, careful not to wake the two women, and grabbed the phone that was continuously going off. In the back of his mind, it registered that the phone was Faye's. Not that it mattered, he answered her phone when she was busy all the time. Not her texts though. He never looked at those. But not many people called. Just her family, really. Well, and Reagan. But she could normally predict who was going to answer the phone and would greet him by name when it was him. Having foresight must be useful. Particularly if it saved the awkward 'who is this' moment when someone unexpected answered the phone.

"Hello," he answered.

"Reese, is Faye there?" Bex's slightly frantic voice came down the line.

He glanced to the side, but both women were completely out still. "She's asleep."

"At this time?" Bex seemed surprised. He wasn't sure he blamed her. Faye was an early riser.

"It's only just gone seven, Bex," he told her, having checked the time on his own phone which had been lying next to Faye's.

"Oh, right yes. Sorry, Fi's had me up since the crack of dawn."

"It's still dark," he pointed out, and could have sworn he heard Bex scowl down the line.

"You know what I mean."

"Sorry, yes, I do. But Faye's still asleep. We had a late night."

"Anything fun?" Bex asked, despite herself. He held back a laugh. That was so like Bex. They both knew she'd called for a reason. With a young child now, there wasn't any chance she'd waste the time with a phone call at seven am. Even so, she was asking after their social life. He supposed it came from knowing them as a couple for so long. He guess she'd have get used to thinking of them as more now.

"Yes, very," he replied truthfully.

Soft hands touched his back, followed by kisses peppered over his shoulder. "Morning," Penny whispered, and Reese smiled to himself. After the night before, she seemed a lot more rested than she had before. But that was good as far as he was concerned. Anything that had either of his mates happier was good in his book.

"Good." The word was followed by silence, which made him wonder just how bad whatever Bex had to say actually was. He stayed quiet, too worried by what it might mean to say anymore. "They found them."

"Where are they?" he asked, not at all surprised by

the subject of the phone call. Nor by the fact Bex had assumed Faye had already told him about their call the previous night. Penny rested her head against his shoulder, listening intently. He didn't mind, neither of them would hide anything from her. She was their mate, it was all about being open.

"The abandoned mill," Bex said.

Reese's blood turned to ice. They'd played there as children. As had a lot of the other paranormals they'd known over the years. If that was where the hunters had set up shop, then it boded very ill for the community as a whole. He hoped people had stopped letting their children head out that way, but he doubted it. The mill was too intriguing for that. No one knew who it belonged to, and children had always made up stories to go with it, ranging from evil vampires, to fairy tale like beasts.

"Are you sure?" he asked eventually.

"Yes." Bex's voice sounded small, and scared, and he wondered whether she'd taken Fiona up there. He doubted it. She was probably still too worried about the little girl getting kidnapped again. Hell, he was worried about the little girl getting kidnapped again. She seemed to have come out of last time alright, but that was probably something to do with Mia finding her. There was something comforting about a family presence, he was sure.

"Okay, we'll get on it as soon as Faye's awake."

"Thank you," she responded, breathing a sigh of relief that was audible down the line.

"And Bex?"

"Hmm?"

"Keep you and Fi safe. Maybe go stay with Mia and Felix or something?"

This time, Bex laughed. "And the house where my sister managed to get herself drugged by a potion *and* didn't notice, is safe from the hunters?"

"I suppose you may have a point. But it's another two people about to watch after Fi. Three if Felix's sister is about."

"I hardly think Autumn is the right role model for a four year old." At least Bex sounded amused now. Though she did have a point. The stories Felix had told about his younger sister didn't exactly paint her in the best light. She was trouble with a capital t, and that was even without their father's search for a husband to deal with. Apparently he was an old school dryad who believed marriage would sort his wayward daughter out.

"True, but at the moment, what's more important? Her safety? Or the impression that a few days with an off the rails dryad will do?"

"Good point. I suppose so long as Autumn doesn't take her on one of her jobs, it'll be fine."

"Somehow, I doubt she'd do that. A four year old would probably slow the process down."

"You'd think," Bex admitted, before slipping into silence.

"You okay?" he asked, after what seemed like too long. He was worried about his sister-in-law. It hadn't been an easy year for her. Hell, it hadn't been an easy four years for her. It was still beyond him how she'd been able to keep a child a secret for so long. If he had a daughter, he'd be shouting about her from the rooftops.

"Sorry, just thinking. You're right, I should call Mia."

"Or Fiona's father," he suggested, hoping she'd at least drop a hint as to who the man was. They were all curious. Bex laughed.

"I wouldn't tell you that, even if I could. I'd end up with my father and two brother-in-laws hunting the poor man down."

"Hardly a poor man. He abandoned you and Fi."

"He doesn't *know* about Fi, Reese."

He found her choice of words interesting. It was

almost like she did know who the girl's father was. There was definitely a certainty to what she was saying.

"Can you ask..." Penny whispered, trailing off. Reese nodded once. It may be an odd question to ask, but if it put his mate at ease, then it was definitely worth it.

"Is there any chance her father is a necromancer?" he asked, anxiously waiting for Bex's response.

"What?"

"A necromancer. You know, purple magic, raising the dead and generally being a bit sinister?"

"I know what a necromancer is, I just don't know why you'd even think that." She sounded a little defensive, but he put it down to him prying into her personal life.

"Just something that crossed my mind," he said with a shrug, and heard Penny's accompanying disappointed sigh.

"No, he was a shifter."

"Thank you for telling me, Bex," he said down the line. He was truly grateful that he'd told her, and not just because he'd felt Penny relaxing against him. But also, because it meant that, when the time came, he could help his niece with the shifting side of things. That reassured him a lot.

"No problem, but please, keep it between us. I'm not sure why you want to know, but there'll be a good reason."

"I can't hide things from my mate," he replied, carefully omitting reference to Penny. That was Faye's place to tell her family. Or maybe both of their places.

"Nor would I expect you to. But my parents, and Mia? Please don't tell them. I'm not ready for the questions yet."

"You got it, Bex. Secret is safe with me," he reassured her.

"Thank you." A shout came in the background, and he smiled knowing Fiona was up and about. He couldn't wait to have a family. It was something he hadn't let himself think about other than in the darkness of night. And then it'd just made him down. But now, it might actually be a possibility. "I need to go," Bex added.

"I guessed. I'll let you know how we get on."

"Thanks," she replied. "See you soon, Reese."

"See you soon," he replied.

The dial tone sounded, and he pulled the phone away from his ear, twisting his head around so he was facing Penny. He kissed her softly.

"Morning," he said.

"Morning," she replied. "So that was Bex?"

He nodded.

"Bex called?" a sleepy voice asked from the bed, and the two of them turned to see Faye lazily rubbing her eyes.

"Yes."

"And?" Faye asked, looking a little more awake by the second.

"We need to go to the old abandoned mill," he told her. She frowned as she tried to process it.

"That's where the hunters are?"

"Apparently." He shrugged.

Faye swung her legs around and jumped to her feet the moment her feet hit the floor. "We should get going then."

16

THE MILL LOOMED ABOVE THEM, making Faye shiver. It was even more decrepit than she remembered. Maybe some young witches had used the area for some sparring. It certainly looked like there were some burn marks on the walls. She couldn't really talk, those of them who had powers had done the same when they were children, though they'd been more careful not to leave marks. People were probably a little bit more dismissive of anomalies now.

She slipped her left hand into Reese's, and her right into Penny's, loving having her mates on each side, there was a complete feeling about it that was unbelievably right to her. She guessed it was because their bonds were sealed now.

"I don't like this place anymore," she muttered.

"Me neither," Reese returned.

"It is a little creepy," Penny said, and they both turned to her. "Though I can see why you guys liked it."

"Didn't you have anything like this as a child?" Faye asked.

"I don't really remember my childhood. Even after I was five, there don't seem to be many more memories. I'm not sure where they even went. Maybe it's just part of the banshee curse? Not knowing who you are." Her voice cracked at the end, and if they hadn't been about to walk into what they thought was a prison, Faye would have pulled her into her arms and offered her the comfort she clearly desperately needed.

"I'm sorry," Reese said.

"Don't be. It was bad luck is all. It's not even the banshee that cursed me's fault. How were they to know I was in the vicinity? It's not like we can control when we scream."

"Can't you?" Faye frowned.

"Well, I guess we can, but not the warning screams. They just come when there's something to warn about."

"What was yesterday's about? Do you know?"

Faye was glad Reese had asked, she was wondering the same thing.

"This, I assume." Penny waved her free hand in the direction of the mill in front of them. "It's leaving me feeling very uneasy."

"Is that normal?"

"I have no idea. I haven't spent a lot of time exploring my powers. I've never really wanted to. Everyone seems to alienate us regardless of what we do. I never wanted to make that worse, so didn't try to work anything out."

"But now you want to?" Faye asked, squeezing the other woman's hand gently.

"I think so. I'm not sure. I already feel a little more at ease with them than I did before. Which is something, I guess." She shrugged, but her expression was open, and Faye knew she was telling the truth. She was just glad that Penny felt at ease enough to talk to them about it.

"Whenever you're ready, we're here," Reese said as Faye nodded in agreement.

"Thank you, guys. But that's not helping us get into the mill."

"True, but I don't really want to go in there," Faye admitted quietly.

"No, me neither, but I guess we're going to have

to," Penny added, before dropping Faye's hand and making her way towards the broken doorway. Not wanting to leave her to face whatever was in there alone, Faye hurried to follow, with Reese close behind. At least they were in this together.

The inside of the mill was even worse than the outside, and it smelled of damp and mildew. Never a great combination. Even less so when there were allegedly prisoners in here. Faye couldn't imagine this was a nice place to be trapped, no matter by who.

They crept through the hallways, following their instincts on where to go. She still wasn't sure about this. How were they actually going to tell if they were going in the right direction? Though she should be thankful she had Reese's in built sense of direction, and Penny's warning system. Even so, her magic was crackling beneath her skin, ready to be used at any moment. It was an odd feeling. She'd never felt it like this before. Her powers had always been tending towards the weak side, with just some intricate capabilities that made it seem like she had more than she really did. For which she was grateful, really. It made the issue much easier to hide.

"Wait," Penny whispered, holding out her arm in order to stop them going any further. They came to a halt, and Penny strained her ears, trying to her whatever it was that'd tipped Penny off. Unfortunately, she heard nothing, though that was maybe because she was using some of her other senses to avoid the things they didn't want to be near.

"What is it?" Reese whispered.

"I'm not sure, something's just telling me we need to stop."

Faye nodded. She'd trust her mates. Both of them. Either of them. They waited for a few more moments before Penny waved them forward, but motioned for them to crouch low. Moments later, the wall tapered off, turning into a shorter one that only came up to Faye's waist. Or it would have done if she'd been standing up.

Voices came from over the wall, and she sucked in a nervous breath. They were too far away, or too muffled at the very least, for her to be able to tell what they were saying, but at this point, she really didn't care. She just wanted to get past them and onto rescuing whoever was down there.

Saying that, she wasn't entirely sure she liked the idea of leaving any of the hunters about. All they'd do then was hurt someone else. Maybe they should have called the Council after all, they'd at least had the manpower to deal with the situation, even if they chose to ignore it.

Penny called them to a halt again, before motioning them on wards again, and down an equally depleted corridor. Why couldn't the bad guys choose a nice comfy stately home to make their lair in or something? It'd be much nicer to sneak around in.

What on earth was she thinking that for? Why would she want to sneak around anywhere more than she had to. It wasn't even like she wanted to sneak about this time. It was through necessity, and doing it for her sister that had her still here.

"I think we're nearly there," Penny whispered. Faye just nodded. There wasn't really anything else she could say to that. Except that she hoped Penny was right. It would mean they could get out of there soon.

A steel door loomed before them. Completely out of place in the run down mill. It made no sense. Or it did make sense, if the place really was being used by the hunters.

"How are we going to get it open?" Penny sounded a little bit panicked.

"Let me," Faye replied. She wasn't completely sure that she could do it, but it was worth a try. If she couldn't manage, then at least she'd tried. She'd still be embarrassed though. Putting her hand against the lock, she sent sparks into it, hoping they'd turn the levers inside it. There was a loud click, and she breathed a sigh of relief. Being with Penny and Reese really had unlocked something within her. Just one of the many good things that had happened as a result. Other than having two people she loved in her life.

She glanced at the red-head as subtly as she could. Did she love her? She supposed she would. Soon. Probably very soon. Though right now, the feelings very much verged on just major like.

"Ready?" she asked them both. They nodded, and Reese pushed open the big metal door, letting the three of them slip inside.

The first thing Faye noticed was the smell. It was rotting meat and sewage, making awful images of what could happen in here flash through her mind. She tried to push them away. They'd give her night-mares if she wasn't careful. Though at least she could be comforted through the night if she did. The people that were down here, not so much. They were probably far more traumatised than she was.

A groan of discomfort came from the left, and she automatically turned that way, making her way hastily in the direction of the sound. When she reached the person who'd made it, she gagged, almost losing the little she'd eaten for breakfast. No person should be degraded to this point. Because now, it was clear where the rotting meat smell was coming from. The man's leg was rotting away, and the stench was unbelievable.

"We need Mia," Faye muttered, making her way over to the man and unlocking the shackles around his wrists. He groaned again, but was barely conscious. He probably didn't even notice they were there.

"We could call her?" Reese suggested. Faye shook her head.

"Too loud. Can you fly to her? Bring her, and Felix. And get them to alert the Council. This is far bigger than we thought, we can't keep them in the dark any longer." He nodded once.

"Want me to get the Shifter Council involved?"

She shook her head. "There's no point. They don't have the jurisdiction, and you know it."

"True."

"What are the Councils?" Penny asked, looking confused, and more than a little ill.

"Our ruling bodies," Faye answered, looking away from her and back at the man. She contemplated trying to use her magic to heal him, but she wasn't sure she trusted herself to do something like that. Not without practice on less serious injuries first. "It's okay, you're safe now," she told the man, despite knowing the words might not be true.

"I'll get Mia," Reese said, transforming into a bird in front of them. Faye didn't even bat an eyelid, she'd seen him transform enough times by now for it not to affect her. Penny, on the other hand, stood transfixed.

"I need a hand moving him," she said to the other woman after Reese had flown off. Penny nodded, and lifted the man's shoulders. Between them, they moved him slowly back into the slightly cleaner area. It wasn't much, but anything that helped was better than chained to the wall.

Faye just wished they could move faster, but there was no chance of that, not without injuring the people that were down here. In total, the two of them found six people, one of whom seemed to be on just about their last breath, Faye hoped they could hold on for just a little longer. But the worst one, was the teenage girl. She was probably about fifteen, and far too young to be subjected to what-ever torture had left so many long slices along her skin. It was disgusting what they'd done to these people.

"What do we do now?" Penny whispered. She'd pulled Faye off to the side, out of earshot of the people they'd found in the dungeon. Not that any of them were conscious enough to be paying any attention. "We can't sneak them all past the guards, we're just not going to have enough time."

"You're right." Faye pushed a hand over her face, trying to work out what the best solution was. "We just need to stall, I guess." She swallowed a lump in her throat.

"Do you think you can do it?" Penny asked.

"I'm not so sure," Faye responded. She could try, but if she failed, then she'd already tipped their hand. Which was definitely no good.

"I think I can."

"Are you sure?"

"You know I said I'd never tried any of my other powers?"

Faye nodded. "Yes."

"Well, that's not entirely true. I once came across a man with a young girl. And I screamed to paralyse him."

"Did it work?" Faye asked, curious and just a little intimidated by her mate.

"Yes, but it felt awful. I'd hoped never to do it again."

"Then don't," Faye insisted, placing a hand on the other woman's arm. "Don't put yourself through that."

"This is a worthwhile cause, and you know it. Just, do me a favour?"

"Anything," she promised instantly.

"Cover your ears, and keep them that way until I come back."

Faye nodded. And Penny smiled weakly, leaning over and kissing her on the cheek.

"I'll be back soon."

She watched as the red-head left, and quickly checked on each of the people they'd found. Thankfully, they all seemed to be hanging on, even the one who seemed close to death. "Just a little longer," Faye promised. She clamped her hands over her ears just as a piercing scream rang out through the building.

17

PENNY NESTLED into Reese's arms even more. She was shaking with the exertion her scream had taken. She'd never practiced with her powers, which meant she didn't know how to do it without having to expend a lot of power. Which definitely wasn't ideal, but the plan had worked. The guards had been frozen, and even now, were being taken away by the Council, who finally seemed to be taking the hunter problem seriously.

From what Reese and Faye had told her, it had seemed to be going on for a while. Though she supposed it was still going on technically. There was almost certainly no one important at the mill, which meant they were all still at large, including the man who'd kidnapped Faye's older sister. It was a shame no one had seemed to be able to do anything about tracking him down. Though maybe with the Council involved, it might be easier now.

"Are you okay?" Faye asked, reaching out and stroking Penny's hair slightly. It didn't stop the shivering, but having both of her mates touching her, was making a difference. There was something special about the two of them, that was for certain.

"B-b-been better," she stammered through her chattering teeth.

"Is there anything we can do to help?"

"Name it, and we'll do it, Penny," Reese added.

"I-is everyone okay?" That was the most important thought in Penny's head. The people they'd found really weren't in a good way, and she needed to know they'd been in time to save them.

"We think so. A couple of people are still unconscious. The man with the leg has been seen to by Mia. He might need to lose it, but that's going to depend on what he is. He might be lucky and be a paranormal that can grow it back after the infections been cleared."

"I thought paranormals weren't supposed to get infections." Reese frowned.

"I guess we can if the situation is particularly dire?" Faye grimaced.

"And the others?" Penny prompted, starting to feel a bit stronger already.

"The teenager isn't awake yet. But one of the women is. I think she's a banshee."

"You do?" Penny perked up at that. She'd never met another of her kind before. And even if she was in bad shape, if it meant she could get to know her soon, it would be worth it.

"Yes, she's giving off the same vibe as you do. Her name is Carmen too." Faye and Reese's eyes met, and understanding dawned on Penny.

"You mean..."

"I hope so. But we'll worry about that later. The Council's here now, there's very little else we can do." Faye trailed her hand down Penny's cheek, and she leaned into the blonde's touch.

"Can we go home?" Penny asked weakly.

"Did you just call ours, home?" A wide smile spread over Faye's face.

"Erm..."

"You did! I heard it. Didn't you, Reese?"

"I sure did, yes." He kissed the top of Penny's head.

"I think it's a great idea. Let's go home."

Thank you for reading *The Banshee's Spark!* Bex's story, *The Lion's Pride*, is coming soon. You can join my mailing list or Facebook reader groups for updates. Until then, why not try one of my other paranormal romance series: https://books2read.com/biteofthepast

ALSO BY LAURA GREENWOOD

Books in the Obscure World

- Ashryn Barker Trilogy (urban fantasy, completed series)
- Grimalkin Academy: Kittens Series (paranormal academy, completed series)
- Grimalkin Academy: Catacombs Trilogy (paranormal academy, completed series)
- City Of Blood Trilogy (urban fantasy)
- Grimalkin Academy: Stakes Trilogy (paranormal academy)
- The Harpy Bounty Hunter Trilogy (urban fantasy)
- The Black Fan (vampire romance)
- Sabre Woods Academy (paranormal academy)
- Scythe Grove Academy (urban fantasy)
- Carnival Of Knives (urban fantasy)

Books in the Forgotten Gods World

- The Queen of Gods Trilogy

(paranormal/mythology romance)
- Forgotten Gods Series
  (paranormal/mythology romance)

The Grimm World

- Grimm Academy Series (fairy tale academy)
- Fate Of The Crown Duology (Arthurian Academy)
- Once Upon An Academy Series (Fairy Tale Academy)

Books in the Paranormal Council Universe

- The Paranormal Council Series (shifter romance, completed series)
- The Fae Queen Of Winter Trilogy (paranormal/fantasy)
- Thornheart Coven Series (witch romance)
- Return Of The Fae Series (paranormal post-apocalyptic, completed series)
- Paranormal Criminal Investigations Series (urban fantasy mystery)
- MatchMater Paranormal Dating App

Series (paranormal romance, completed series)

- The Necromancer Council Trilogy (urban fantasy)
- Standalone Stories From the Paranormal Council Universe

Other Series

- The Apprentice Of Anubis (urban fantasy in an alternate world)
- Untold Tales Series (fantasy fairy tales, completed series)
- The Dragon Duels Trilogy (urban fantasy dystopia)
- ME Contemporary Standalones (contemporary romance)
- Standalones
- Seven Wardens, co-written with Skye MacKinnon (paranormal/fantasy romance, completed series)
- Tales Of Clan Robbins, co-written with L.A. Boruff (urban fantasy Western)
- The Firehouse Feline, co-written with Lacey Carter Andersen & L.A. Boruff (paranormal/urban fantasy romance)

- Kingdom Of Fairytales Snow White, co-written with J.A. Armitage (fantasy fairy tale)

Twin Souls Universe

- Twin Souls Trilogy, co-written with Arizona Tape (paranormal romance, completed series)
- Dragon Soul Series, co-written with Arizona Tape (paranormal romance, completed series)
- The Renegade Dragons Trilogy, co-written with Arizona Tape (paranormal romance, completed series)
- The Vampire Detective Trilogy, co-written with Arizona Tape (urban fantasy mystery, completed series)
- Amethyst's Wand Shop Mysteries Series, co-written with Arizona Tape (urban fantasy)

Mountain Shifters Universe

- Valentine Pride Trilogy, co-written with

L.A. Boruff (paranormal shifter romance, completed series)

- Magic and Metaphysics Academy Trilogy, co-written with L.A. Boruff (paranormal academy, completed series)
- Mountain Shifters Standalones, co-written with L.A. Boruff (paranormal romance)

Audiobooks: www.authorlauragreenwood.co.uk/p/audio.html

ABOUT THE AUTHOR

Laura is a USA Today Bestselling Author of paranormal and fantasy romance. When she's not writing, she can be found drinking ridiculous amounts of tea, trying to resist French Macaroons, and watching the Pitch Perfect trilogy for the hundredth time (at least!)

FOLLOW THE AUTHOR

- Website: www.authorlauragreenwood.co.uk
- Mailing List: www.authorlauragreenwood.co.uk/p/mailing-list-sign-up.html
- Facebook Group: http://facebook.com/groups/theparanormalcouncil
- Facebook Page: http://facebook.com/authorlauragreenwood

- Bookbub: www.bookbub.com/authors/ laura-greenwood
- Instagram: www. instagram.com/authorlauragreenwood
- Twitter: www.twitter.com/lauramg_tdir